In the Morning Light

BA TORTUGA

BA's Cozy Cowboys

If y'all are interested in warm, joyous novels where the cowboys have kids and love saves the day, please check these BA Tortuga books out:

Back in the Saddle

Cowboy Haven

Cowboy in the Crosshairs

Cowboy Logic

Cowboy's Law

In the Morning Light

Ranch Manny

Security Detail: an AusTex novel

The Cowboy Contract

The Cowboy Guardian

The Meaning of Life

Trial by Fire: an AusTex novel

Two Cowboys and a Baby

Two of a Kind

To those of us who finally found our way home. May you find yours.

Also, special thanks to J. You rock, lady.

BA

Chapter One

Austin McPherson wandered through the food stalls at the Sheriff's Posse rodeo grounds in Agua Azul, New Mexico. He had to admit, for such a middle of nowhere desert town, the grounds were nice, with a solid layout and decent gates. Somehow, though, when his buddy David Duran had said he knew a great little rodeo near Las Vegas they could do over the Fourth of July, Austin had thought Nevada, not New Mexico.

"You gonna have a corny dog, Texas?" David asked, and Austin shook his head.

"Nah. I think I'll go for the Frito pie." When in New Mexico...

"They do make it right here, eh?" David beamed at him. "I owe you big for agreeing to come out. The organizers think I'm a big shit now. You saved my butt."

"Yeah? I'll file that one away." Not that he actually kept track of "who owed who" what. They all called on their friends when they needed them. David had needed a bigger rodeo name to draw a crowd this year, and he'd been available. "It's a nice arena."

"I think so. The bulls are coming in local; the space gets a little love each year, so it never gets too beat up."

"Yeah, I can tell. So many of the small arenas get worn down."

"Yeah. That's why we try to get guys in during cowboy Christmas. It's the way to drive the pennies in while folks are having their summers. We always get decent bulls—the Donoghues bring 'em in—but this year we get bulls and a million-dollar cowboy."

"Someone here is that good?" He widened his eyes, but the name shook him. He knew a Donoghue who did rodeos.

"Yeah. They're local, so the bull had to travel less than half an hour. Fresh meat for you."

"And before that I get to sit and digest my Frito pie." He ordered when he stepped up to the window, then looked around at the crowd, just people watching while he waited.

It was your normal New Mexico crowd, really. A little less short-shorts with boots, a little more Santa Fe, but really? Stetsons, Luccheses, Wranglers, button-downs, and big silver buckles—it was like being at home with more green chile.

A couple of little gals went by, wiggling and smiling, and he looked away because it wasn't fair to let them think they had a chance.

Which was when he took the punch to his lungs that almost brought him to his knees. Jim Donoghue.

He'd know that chiseled jaw, the tight ass, the scar on that left cheek from a bullwhip accident years ago—that was his Mr. Right that had ghosted the fuck out of him damn near a year ago.

Austin almost turned on his heel and walked the other way. But then they called him for his food, and after he grabbed it, he found his boots following Jim. He had a piece to say to the man.

Jim was being stopped every few people, and the tall

bastard chatted with each and every one, even as he made his way toward the chutes.

It seemed to take forever to catch him, but finally he was in reach. Austin tossed his Frito pie into the trash can before he reached out to spin Jim around.

"Whoa! Watch it!" Jim turned to glare, and Austin was sure the son of a bitch had said something; he just wasn't sure what that could possibly be.

Austin didn't hear a thing, because Jim had his hands full.

Full of a little baby in a pink sun hat.

"Fuck me."

Chapter Two

J im Donoghue stared down at the pocket cowboy that had stopped him. "Watch your goddamn mouth!"

Austin fucking McPherson. The last little son of a bitch he wanted to see.

"Me? Watch my mouth? Oh, honey, you'd best be glad I lost the ability to talk there for a second or your ears would be melting off." Austin's face was like a thundercloud.

"Shut up, Austin. I mean it. Not here." He wasn't going to do this in front of Rosie, God, and the entire goddamn town. Fuck John and his broken arm anyway.

"Please, Jim, I just need a hand."

"Please, Jim, I need your help this time."

"Please, Jim."

"Please, please, please."

"Not here? When you made it not anywhere for a year? You could have just told me you got someone knocked up, thanks for the good time." Austin could do cutting, for sure.

"Don't be an idiot, McPherson. It's not a good look on you." Like he'd cheated on Austin. At all.

Shit, when he'd discovered his little cousin Modette had gotten herself in trouble, and he knew he was serious about adopting Rosie, he had tried talking to Austin, seeing if he was willing to settle down a little, and Austin had laughed in his face.

"Me?" Austin's voice rose again. "What the hell am I supposed to think?"

"That I adopted a baby." What a jackass.

Sure, he was guilty of just walking away. Of course he was. He'd had a baby coming, a lover that wasn't interested in settling down, and he'd known he couldn't look at Austin and let the beautiful son of a bitch go.

"You—" Austin rocked back on the heels of his boots, blinking hard. "What? Why?"

"Because I wanted a family, McPherson. I told you that. Over and over." And Austin hadn't listened. Over and over. "I'm sorry, man. I have to go. John needs help. He broke his arm."

"Wait."

"Mr. McPherson! Can I have your autograph?" A twelve-ish-year-old kid ran up, and Jim made his escape. To his credit, Austin never turned down the kids.

Hell, Austin never turned anyone down. He loved his job more than anything on earth. Anything. Jim had tried hard to understand that, and he'd had to turn his back on it in the long run. He'd hoped he would just never see the man again except maybe on TV.

He was in love, but this baby had needed him, and, if he was honest, he'd needed Rosie too. She made his life so much fuller. So much more amazing. She gave him purpose beyond raising bulls for guys like Austin to buck off.

He got over near the chutes, eyes searching for his brother, John like a two-year younger carbon copy of him.

"Hey. Hey, little girl." John appeared as if conjured, bending to kiss Rosie on the forehead. "You need me to take her? I need you to be chute boss."

"That's why I'm here." He kissed the top of Rosie's head, and she didn't even make a peep. "Did you know Austin McPherson was here?"

"No sh-kidding?" John raised his eyebrows. "Nope. That would be on Katie. She's the Sheriff's Posse organizer."

"Yeah. Yay. He'll be gone tomorrow. He's pissed at me though, so—"

"Well..." John knew the story, and more than once he'd said Jim should tell the man what had happened. Even if it was in an email or something.

"Shut up."

"Uh-huh. Ghosting is rude, man."

"Don't we have work to do? Aren't we busy in the chutes here?" He knew. He did. He'd just been too fucked up to deal like he ought to have.

"Well, unstrap Rosie and hand her over." John held out his good arm.

Reluctantly, he gave her up. "No taking her up on the chutes."

"Shit. I'm going to sit in the stands where we won't get the dirt and poop, and I'm going to take notes on how it all runs."

He rolled his eyes. Yay. Notes. "Where's my clipboard?"

"With my—your—assistant. It's Laney tonight."

"Good." He worked well with her, and she was an efficient lady. She'd been a barrel racer back when their mom had been too. They were fierce, strong women, and he wouldn't be surprised if he didn't raise one of his own.

He climbed the gate and waved to Laney, who waved right back at him, looking like the rodeo queen she was in a sequined shirt that was pansy purple. "Hey, Jim! How goes?"

"Fine as frog hair, lady. Everyone behaving themselves?"

She shrugged, and the sequins made him a little dizzy. "J993 is being a bitch. He wants out."

"Yeah? Well, he's a jumper, so keep an eye on him. Tie the rope over his pen to keep him down if you have to." A lot of folks had no idea how high a bull could leap. And that was from standing. And if they could get the front of their body over something, the back end would follow. God help them if they got a little room to run...

"Yeah, we might. He's just like a Mexican bean in there. I'm not sure what bit his nutsac."

"Hell if I know. Could just be that he didn't have to travel." They were close to home, so the bulls were all fresh as daisies. "Anything else?"

"Yeah. I need animal medical to look at that chestnut mare, Twister? She's favoring her right foreleg."

"I'm on it. I'll go grab them and have them check her out. If we have to, we won't buck J993, okay? I don't want anyone hurt." Animal or human athlete, either one.

"Got it. And you know we have a celeb, right?"

He rolled his eyes. "I do now." He wished someone had warned him.

"Yeah, nice of them to tell us. I would have had you bring Halitosis."

"Or Boogerbear, right?" He started chuckling, just tickled as all get out. "I guess I could run home real quick and load him up."

"Oh, man. Nah, he deserves his day off."

Boogerbear usually went to bull riding events, not smaller rodeos. He'd earned the time off for cowboy Christmas, which was the time around the Fourth of July, when the smaller rodeos took precedence, and the big shows took a hiatus. He had spent the last few months working at the ranch, and he found he loved it, compared to being on the road. That was John's passion, not his.

"Keep me posted on anything else. I'll be doing prechecks. Everything ready for after the grand entry?" The posse handled that, because it was their show.

"As far as I know. You got the sheep and the calves ready for the kids?" Why on earth John had volunteered them to be the event's stock contractor, he didn't know.

Well, he did know.

John was into Lisa Hanks, one of the organizing committee folks. He was hooked through the balls.

Jim shook his head, heading to turn in some paperwork to the announcer, who was on horseback tonight. Ed Langley was one of the best, up from Texas, but he could do the show in English and Spanish, which the locals loved.

"Hey, Jim. Got roped into replacing John, did you? I heard about his arm. Did they have to surge on it?"

"Yeah, he got trapped between a bull and a trailer door. He's watching the baby. I'm pitch-hitting. You let me know what you need from me."

"You got it. The posse is pretty good. Only one new kid this year and he's just running scores back and forth."

"Yeah? Who's our horseback safety team?"

"Julio Damiano and Hank Long."

"Nice."

He got a keen look. "You see Austin McPherson is here?"

Ugh. Why did everyone keep asking him that? It wasn't like they'd been obvious.

"I did. I ran into him earlier." Yay.

"Ah. Well, he's been riding well, so the crowd ought to love it." He got a slight grin. "Hey, Addie and Dylan and Laura came up with me. You want to have lunch tomorrow before we leave town?"

"Sounds like a plan, but I'll have to see how Miss Thang is doing. This *is* her first rodeo."

"Well, y'all let us know. The kids love to meet babies. You know how that is."

He was learning, yes. Toddlers to preteens seemed fascinated, tweens and teens indifferent. But Ed's kids were just of the right age, and they were well-behaved. And he liked Addie.

"Sounds like a plan. Have a good show, buddy."

"From your mouth to God's ears, my friend."

They just needed an easy event. No injuries. No drama. Please God. Up and down, load, and go home.

He headed back to the chutes, finding the doc and reminding him to look at that mare. She was in from Souther's Rodeo, and he didn't know them, but he wasn't going to buck a hurt horse on his watch. No way.

Lord have mercy, why the fuck did Austin show up here? He loved the son of a bitch—had since he laid eyes on the man in Vegas during an event—but he'd asked, flat out, if Austin would consider settling down. They'd been fucking for years —sometimes once a month, sometimes once a week, sometimes once a quarter. It had always been amazing, but—he needed more.

Now Austin was right here in his lap, wanting answers, and Jim just wasn't sure he had them, or was willing to give them.

He wasn't a rodeo man, not at his core, and he knew that it hadn't been Austin that had changed the day Modette came to him asking for help. But it had been him. At least half of the life he wanted so bad was offered to him that day, and he'd grabbed at it with both hands.

He hadn't known how to tell Austin things, so he'd taken the easy way out.

"Hey, Mr. Donoghue. Great weather tonight, huh?" That was his gate puller.

"Absolutely fabulous." Nice breeze, not a cloud in the sky —it was a perfect New Mexico—

There was an uproar of bull noise, banging, and shouting, and he whirled around just in time to see J993 go over the rail of the bullpens, back feet kicking like crazy.

"Jim! He's out!" Laney hollered. "And he's in the contestant lot."

Oh, fuck him. "Somebody get me a horse and a rope!"

Chapter Three

They all ran to help. That was what cowboys did when the cows, or in this case, one very pissed-off bull, got out. Thirty or forty cowboys and girls hit the contestant parking lot, and damn if car alarms weren't going off like they were in downtown Albuquerque on a Friday night.

Jim Donoghue was a wet dream, moving that horse like a centaur, rope swinging. Austin hadn't seen anything prettier. And God knew, he'd known cowboys in his life. Jim was everything he wanted.

He and David got behind the damn beast, driving him back toward Jim, who was ready if he could just get into range. He'd be damned if the bull didn't change lanes and headed back through another aisle. Then the son of a bitch put his head down and started ramming vehicles.

Starting with Austin's pickup. Which was a rental.

"Motherfuck!"

"That's what you get for double parking that bitch!" David cackled, about the time the bull went in for another ram.

"Fuck off, Duran, and help me!" He waved his arms and

shouted, running at the bull from the side to try to get him to turn.

Of course, that was when the asshole turned to glare at him like it could tell he was a bull rider. Fuck a duck sideways. He was ready to duck behind someone else's truck. Maybe not a rental. Damn it. He was gonna have to call the rent-a-car place about bull damage.

Okay, so that was a little funny.

About the time he was fixin' to pole vault into a random Ford F150, Jim came wheeling around the truck and hooked a loop on the bull's horns.

"I said no, you son of a bitch." Jim tugged the rope hard, spinning the bull's attention.

The bull bellowed, and kicked one more time for good measure, leaving another huge dent in Austin's vehicle. "Christ on a cracker, Donoghue! That's my truck."

"Oops!" Jim's laugh trailed back at him and he rolled his eyes. Asshole. Beautiful asshole.

Jim dragged the bull, snorting and kicking, all the way back to a trailer, loading the big motherfucker up.

"You want me to drive him home, Boss?" A pretty middle-aged lady popped up next to Jim.

"Yeah, if you would. Hell, you'll be back before the team roping is over. Daddy will be waiting for you at the gate."

"You got it."

The bull was losing it in the trailer.

"And have him check out everything, make sure it's nothing medical."

"I'll tell him." She chuckled. "The five-star guest is a little pissed."

Austin rolled his eyes. "Of course I am. That's my truck." They were acting like he wasn't there.

"She's talking about the bull, McPherson."

"Uh-huh."

The lady waved, and she wisely drove off without saying anything.

"So, my truck. Your bull."

Jim's horse picked its way over to him, and Jim peered at his driver's side door. "Shit."

"That's gonna be a bitch to explain," David said, coming to a stop next to him.

He gave David the side-eye. "Beat it, Duran."

David looked up, eyes widening when he realized who was on the horse. "I'm out."

"So, we have insurance, and I'm sure you have insurance, so…"

Oh no. No way was Jim getting off that easy.

"Yeah, well, I'm not gonna be able to drive it anywhere like this."

Jim's eyebrows went up. "Your friend there can give you a ride."

"Duran?" Oh, no. "He came up in a van with three buddies. I don't travel that way." He went for innocent, praying he could pull it off. "I don't even have a hotel room for tonight, buddy. Nothing. And now I can't drive into Albuquerque."

Jim stared at him, brows lowering into a scowl. "I'll see what I can scare up for you. There should be something in Las Vegas."

There wasn't. That was why he'd been ready to drive to Burque. Fourth of July in small towns meant no beds. But he just shrugged, feeling like the cat who had cornered the mouse. "Mmm."

"Don't worry. I'll figure something out. If nothing else, I'll put you in Momma's guest room." Look at that scowl, that little pout. So pretty.

"Uh-huh. I'll see you at your truck with my go bag after the event." He stalked off like he was still pissed off, but really, he didn't want to give Jim time to protest. He had a way in, and he was fixin' to catch it like a gold ring.

The man might ghost him, but Jim would never strand someone at a rodeo. Especially not one where everyone knew him.

Austin grinned. He would dine out on this one for ages.

But right now he had to go get ready. He had to ride at least two bulls tonight and live up to his reputation.

The rodeo had been an utter shitshow.

They'd had three wrecks. Not one of the team ropers did their jobs. McPherson won the bull riding. And worst of all, he'd never even thought of the utter hysteria that fireworks would put in his baby girl's soul. He had never heard a scream like she'd given out while he was helping load up, and he had to admit, he'd run, grabbing her from John, wrapping her up, and taking her to his truck.

When Austin appeared, it was almost a relief, because he wanted out.

"Shit, man, is she sick?" Austin was right there, concern on his face. No mockery at all.

"The fireworks, man. Get in so we can go? John's got help." He didn't even hesitate. He needed to get her out of here.

"Sure." Just like that, Austin was in his truck, gear stowed. "Hit it."

So he did. He'd texted everyone who could help get John home with their animals, called in favors. He turned the radio on, not loud, but enough to help cover the noise, and put on something soothing. Rosie did love King George Strait's baritone.

They were five miles away before Rosie started to hiccup, then her desperate cries became tiny sobs.

"They really set her off, huh?" Austin asked quietly.

"She's only three months old. I was fucking stupid. I never thought." Poor baby ears.

"Oh, man. That's harsh. If you need to stop and let me sit back there with her, or you want me to drive…"

"It's not too far, man. We're just up the way." That was really decent, though.

"So this is really local for you." Austin sounded utterly shocked.

"Yeah." How fucked up was it that they'd been sleeping together for what? Ten years? And Austin didn't know where he lived? Jesus, what kind of relationship was this?

He guessed it wasn't one. He'd just left the man without an explanation and then not answered his calls.

"Well, then I don't feel so bad about dogging you to take me home with you and deal with my rental." Austin winked over at him.

Fuck, it wasn't like he could dump the guy on Momma. Not now. "Yeah. I got a futon in the office. My guest room turned into a little girl's room."

"I've had worse."

He breathed a little sigh of relief. At least Austin wasn't pushing to sleep in his bed.

Yet.

He pulled up in front of his ranch house and killed the engine, letting the silence wash over him a second.

Even with Austin in the car, this was home, and Jim felt himself relaxed, deep in his gut. The adobe was sprawling, the vigas sticking out to drain the rain off the flat roof. The roses were still mid-sized, but they were growing, and when Rosie was big enough to ride a bike on the driveway, they'd be flourishing. He had a bright purple door to ward off evil spirits, and all the shutters were turquoise.

"It's a nice place," Austin murmured, and he nodded. It was. It was the best place. Sand and pines, mountains and sage.

When he looked in the rearview, Rosie was asleep. Thank God. What had he been thinking? Taking her to a rodeo like it was nothing? God, he wasn't the best daddy alive, was he?

"Hey." Austin touched his arm. "We all started going to rodeos when we were her age, man. So now you know about the fireworks and know better."

"Right. Baby headphones. It's got to be a thing." He'd order some from Amazon.

"Good deal." Austin got out, grabbing his bag and waiting while he pulled Rosie out of her car seat. "So is this you and your brother and folks, or just you?"

"This house is just mine. John lives where those lights are to the east. The folks live a little farther off the main road. Come on in." They had enough land to have privacy and family, altogether.

He eased Rosie's chair from its base and lifted her, careful not to wake her up. She'd have a bottle and go down, hopefully, and forget about the scary fireworks.

Austin followed him, staying quiet, which was a feat, because he could damn well feel the man vibrating with questions.

He opened the door, letting them in to the tiled foyer. "I'll show you where to drop your stuff. Come on."

The bedrooms and the whole baths were down one hall. "Here's the office and the bathroom. I'm going to take my work clothes off. I'm dusty."

And he needed to sit for a second with his thoughts and make things work.

"Thanks." Austin didn't say another word, just headed

into the bathroom. He was a little shocked by that too. Austin wasn't known for circumspection.

Jim went to his bedroom and stripped down, giving himself a spit bath before putting on a loose pair of jeans and a t-shirt. Not too casual, not too tight.

Rosie was beginning to wake up, her lips pursed and working, looking for something to suck.

He eased her pacifier into her lips, smiling down at her. "Hey, sweet baby. I love you. Give me two shakes, and I'll feed you." She sucked hard, and he had to laugh. She was working out her shit. "I know! That was your first rodeo. Can you believe it? It was an eventful one too. Escapee bull. McPherson. Uncle John's arm. Fireworks. Nuts."

She watched him, eyes following his movements, but she was calm now. Like she knew she was home and safe and about to get fed.

"That's right. Now we'll have a nice bath, a bottle, a snuggle, and tomorrow it'll be Sunday."

He stripped her down, washing her with a wet, warm cloth, singing to her as he got the dust off.

Then he changed her, checked his shirt for goo – babies came with a shitton of goo and took her out to get her fed. He was feeling way more steady. Ready for the battle to come.

She settled into her little bouncy chair, cooing and smiling as she watched him.

"That's my girl." He sang to her a little, moving between fridge and microwave. When he looked up, Austin stood in the doorway, watching them.

"Hey. Coke? Beer? Water?" He was going to stay perfectly calm, breathe through his nose.

"If you don't mind, I could use a beer. Easier on the belly than a pain pill." Austin gave him a wry smile, and he felt his shoulders relax some. Looked like they were having a truce for whatever reason. He'd take it.

"I got Tecate, Corona, and Bud Light." He even had limes.

"Corona is good. You know I like it. Can I help with anything?"

He glanced sideways at Austin, blowing out a breath. "Why are you being so nice?"

"Well…" Austin drawled the word out, and he heard the Texas there, knew what that inflection meant. Austin was far from calm. "You got your kid right here. You've had a shit night, and it's late. And I got to admit, I'm processing how you have all this life I don't know about. Like not one bit."

"Believe it or not, I was just thinking the same thing." He grabbed two beers, checked the bottle, and found a lime. "Here, cut you a wedge. Knives are in the block."

"Got it." Austin cut the lime into wedges, then popped both beers and put lime wedges in the mouths of the bottles.

Jim got Rosie to eating, taking her over to his recliner for her supper. "Have a seat, man."

"Thanks." Austin came to sit across from him on the couch. "This is a nice place."

"Thank you. I built it about eight years ago when my grandfather left me this land."

"I can't believe I've never seen it." Austin was watching him, though, not looking around the front room. He felt a little pinned down.

"I can't believe we never talked about…anything important." Had they ever had a deep conversation? Talked about anything but rodeo, food, and fucking?

"Yeah." Austin grinned suddenly. "You're still smoking hot, though."

"Shut up, butthead." He chuckled though, because to be honest, Austin was too. Austin was still the finest man he'd ever seen—deep laugh lines, a warm smile, and a little hard body. Those eyes, pale gray but not icy, were just fascinating, and the dark hair was just starting to show a few strands of gray early on.

It was a good look.

"So tell me what happened? If she's not yours."

"My cousin got in trouble, and she was telling me what had happened. She was on summer break before her freshman year at college, had a drunken fling, and the rubber broke. She wasn't even sure where the guy was from. She didn't want to raise a baby. I did." It really was as simple as that. He'd paid the medical expenses, she'd signed over all her rights, and Rosie had a daddy that wanted her.

"I—shit, man, I know you talked about kids, but—"

"But what? You thought I was joking?"

"No." Austin's expression went blank and smooth like it did when he was uncomfortable. "I just figured that wasn't an option for guys like us."

"Well, it is. It was an option for me. I talked to you—trying to feel you out—when I found out. It's okay. You aren't interested in settling down, and I wanted a family of my own." He tried for a smile, but he didn't have one, so he looked down at the baby in his arms, who was starting to doze instead of eat, just idly playing with the nipple.

"I—Well. Congratulations, honey. She's gorgeous." That was closed off, just like Austin always was when he was really damn mad. Like Austin had a right to be. Asshole. Normally he would just leave it be, but this time he couldn't.

"Don't you get all pissy with me. I should have told you. That's on me. But you would have walked away as fast as you could if I had."

Austin gave him a long look, and it was damn near unreadable. "Sure. That's me. Walkaway Joe."

"What?" His own temper was holding on like a piece of barbed wire that was fixin' to let loose. "Shit, man. I called you the day I found out. You freaked on me when I mentioned settling down, making a home together. This isn't a love affair; it was a pair of guys with more chemistry than is reasonable getting it on. The fact that I wanted to do something different? That's on me. You haven't changed your spots."

That hit finally, and Austin's jaw tightened, his eyes flashing fire. "You got a hell of a lot of nerve assuming you know what my spots even look like. You got your rocks off with a fuck the rodeo cowboy fantasy and you never tried to go any deeper than that. Don't you tell me."

Whoa. Whoa! "That wasn't intended as an insult, man. I meant that you didn't change, I did. I got my rocks off once a quarter, and it was amazing. I needed something for the other three hundred and sixty days a year." He shrugged, suddenly unwilling to fight about it anymore. What was he supposed to say? *I fell in love, and I realized that even that wasn't enough to fill up the empty spaces?* God, he was a shitty person. Falling in love was supposed to be everything, and he just couldn't make those stolen nights stretch to cover the endless lonely days. "I should have said something. I just couldn't. I'm sorry."

Austin's shoulders sagged. "Yeah. Yeah, I'm sorry too, honey. Do you have the stuff for me to have a sandwich before we say goodnight? I didn't get much before I rode."

"Oh good Lord." Jim rolled his eyes and stood. "You know I'll feed you. I haven't eaten either. You want some green chile chicken casserole? It's leftover, but it's good."

"That sounds like a plan." He got a ghost of Austin's megawatt smile. "Thanks, honey."

"No worries." Rosie could go in her little pack and play while they ate, and then he'd put her to bed. "Come on. I think I even have extra tortillas to go with."

They could at least have a meal together, and if he wanted to pretend this was the life he could have had for half an hour, well, sue him.

Chapter Five

Austin tucked his wallet into his jeans and went hunting for Jim.

It was time to get on the road, get out of Jim's house. This so-very New Mexico adobe. He could feel Jim soaked into the entire space – from the nichos in the walls holding pictures of Rosie to the huge wood beams in the ceilings. This wasn't a house. This was Jim's *home*. There wasn't any place in his life now for Austin. That was clear as glass. A cowboy had to know when to ride away, and it was time.

He'd tossed and turned on that damn futon all night trying to justify staying around and fighting about it, but Jim didn't want him, even if he wanted Jim so bad it liked to kill him.

So.

He grabbed his hat, then headed out to the bright blue kitchen, damn near wincing at the sun that poured in. All he needed was his boots and a ride back to the arena. Except there was no Jim. Not in the kitchen drinking coffee, not in the front room, or even on the screened in back porch, which had a nice swing and a hell of a view, right up into the mountains.

Shit, he wasn't up that early. Was Jim just sleeping in? He was willing to buy breakfast, even.

So he put his boots down hard heading down the back hall to the master bedroom he'd never seen, and when he knocked, the door swung open. Austin had a head of steam, so he just bulldozed in. "Damn it, Jim, wake up—"

The pinewood bed was made with a soft-looking dark green comforter, a light tan dress shirt laid out on it.

That isn't what held his attention, though. Not even a little.

What caught him was the huge dresser that matched the bed, a big old mirror hanging above it. The mirror was stuffed with so many pieces of paper that Austin couldn't see himself. Except he could. There were pictures of him riding. Pictures of him and Jim all over the country, smiling, arms around each other. There were tickets to rodeos and bull ridings stuffed between the wood and glass, and clippings from the Rodeo News taped here and there. A signed daysheet from his million-dollar win hung on the lowest spot. And right there on the dresser top next to a picture of little Rosie set in a gilded frame, was the silver buckle from that win, the one he'd handed Jim and said the man had inspired him to greatness.

Well, he'd be damned.

This heat flooded down his spine, swirled in his groin for a second, then climbed up his belly toward his cheeks. This wasn't someone who'd moved on. This wasn't a man who'd done forgot him.

When he looked a little closer, there were articles and pictures aplenty from the past year. Jim may have "given him up" but he still wanted, didn't he?

Austin took one more look, then tiptoed out of the bedroom and went to grab his bag from where he'd left it by the front door. Nope. Not leaving today. He took that and his wallet and put them back in the office. He was staying a bit. If

Jim was still that invested in him, well... Then he reckoned this was worth fighting over.

Jim just needed to learn to be more direct, was all. Sometimes you had to hit him over the head pretty hard.

Austin wandered out toward the well-kept barns to find Jim, and sure enough, there he was, that baby in a deal against his chest, singing as he fed the goats.

Goats. Lord help him.

"Hey. You need a hand, honey?"

Jim looked over to him, and fuck if that grin wasn't the sweetest thing he'd ever seen. "Sure. I was just finishing up with the feeding, but I still need to make sure everyone's got water. Miss Rosie likes to watch the chickens."

"Well, I can work a hose. Point me and shoot me." He was a rare bull rider. He'd grown up on a ranch. Nothing big like this, but a ranch nonetheless.

"The spigot is there, and if you'll just fill these two tanks, I'd appreciate it. You sleep okay?" That baby looked adorable with her pink cotton hat, little hands fisted in Jim's work shirt.

"I did. I got a bruise the size of a pancake on my hip, but it just kept me from rolling over to that side." He winked, then whistled while he did his thing, laughing when it made little Rosie sing with him.

"Ah-ya-ya-ya!"

"Listen to her!"

"I know. God help me when she learns to talk. Right now she just loves musical anything."

"Yeah? Do you sing to her?" He couldn't remember if he'd ever heard Jim sing or not before this morning. He had a nice tenor. Austin was a baritone himself.

"All the time. She spends most of her time with me here."

"Yeah? Your folks don't take her all the time?" He knew Jim had a tight-knit family. They seemed like the kind who would love to have babies around.

"Oh, they get their grandbaby time, but she's a daddy's girl, and I miss her when she's gone." Jim winked at him, those pretty eyes twinkling from under his gimme cap.

"She's cute as a button." He might not have ever even pondered kids, but he liked them. He was a cowboy. It was in his DNA.

"She is. She was tiny when she was born—just barely five pounds. I couldn't believe it."

"Wow." He moved a little closer to peer down at her. Such a little one.

"She's three months now." Jim glanced over at him, smiled. "You see why I had to adopt her. I saw the ultrasound photos, and my heart knew."

"I had no idea this was what you meant all those times, honey." He dared to touch her downy cheek. His finger was huge – huge compared to her little face. "What do you want for breakfast? I can rustle something up."

"Yeah? I got eggs, bacon, pancake stuff...you name it."

"I'll go hunt." He grinned, encouraged that Jim wasn't shoving him out the door. Not that he was going yet. Not a bit.

Jim nodded. "I'll be right in. I just need to finish up out here."

"Good deal. No rush." He would do all his insurance shit this morning but it was early for that now. He headed into the kitchen, wondering what this room would tell him about Jim. Austin felt a little like a detective, digging for clues.

Jim's house was neat, the yellow and bright blue kitchen baby-proofed. The eat-in kitchen had a brand-new high chair, a homemade table and chairs – one of Jim's granny's table-cloths making the whole room comfy.

Nice.

He opened cabinets and found a batter bowl, then the pancake mix. The fridge yielded bacon, eggs, and milk. Boom.

Austin would splurge this morning since he wasn't back on the big show circuit until late August.

The fridge had a couple of baby bottles, and there was precious little sweeter than the sight of a bottle with purple flowers next to a mostly empty coffee mug that said "World's Best Daddy" on it. Even a roughstock dickhead like him could understand why Jim wanted this. He hadn't lied when he told Jim that guys like him didn't get things like that in life.

But dammit, he wanted Jim, Jim wanted him, and he knew that they deserved to work this shit out.

So he got bacon going, baking it in the little toaster oven to render the grease out and get it crispy, then he whipped up pancake batter. There was a griddle plate on the stove, which was a fancy-ass model. So all he had to do was oil it.

Jim came in and got Rosie out of her carrier and took her hat off. "It smells good in here."

"Bacon always works, right?"

Jim raised his eyebrows. "You're eating bacon?"

"I have a month to eat and a month to lose whatever I gain." He winked, patting his belly, which was too skinny right now, really.

"There you go." Jim chuckled and put the baby on the floor in a little portable bed thing. "Bacon is proof God loves us."

"You know it, honey." He moved close, letting Jim feel him a little. He wanted to rev them up some. He did love that low, husky sound, the way Jim's breath caught.

"Let me get the syrup and butter out." Jim moved away, but he wasn't running. He was buzzing, Austin could tell.

"You got the good syrup, honey?"

"I do. From Vermont, even."

"Good deal. Why waste the calories on the crap?" He peeked in at Rosie, who seemed to be asleep.

"Exactly." Jim grabbed his cup off the table. "You want coffee?"

"Please. I could use some caffeine." He watched that tall, lean form move around the kitchen, and that ass was still tight as a drawn bow, and he managed to save the pancakes before he burned them, because *damn*.

"No problem. I know how you take it." Jim poured two mugs, gave him some milk.

"You remember." He let their fingers touch when he grabbed his cup. He wasn't above using every little weapon at his disposal. Not one bit. He wasn't the only one that felt that shock, the electricity sharp between them.

No, when Jim looked at him, those pupils were blown, his cheeks flying flags of color. He wanted a kiss, but Austin knew he hadn't earned it yet. Jim had ghosted him, but he hadn't been listening. At all. If he had, he might have known.

In hindsight, Jim had asked him for hope, and he'd laughed in his lover's face. Hell, he'd let himself be satisfied with a hook up, every now and again. He should have fought harder to feel worthy of Jim and maybe he would have been. Not that they didn't have shit to talk about.

"Flip the pancakes." Jim pinked for him, gave him a half-grin.

He flipped. And pulled out the bacon. Lord have mercy, he might have been hungry. He'd made enough for a working.

"This is amazing. I'd call John to join us, but—" Jim shrugged uncomfortably, and Austin thought about losing his temper, snarling about how he didn't need any asshole being ashamed of him, when Jim continued with, "—I'm not feeling like sharing."

His shoulders relaxed. "We'll make him a plate he can have later, huh?" He needed to stop jumping to conclusions with both boots on. "I'm not really in a share-y place right now either."

Jim nodded once, just a dip of the chin, but it felt like it meant something important.

So he poured out the rest of the batter, keeping the made pancakes in a metal pie pan he'd found, letting the heat from the stove keep them warm. And he sang a little to Miss Rosie, running through some old cowboy tunes.

Her now wide-awake, little blue eyes followed him, and she cooed and kicked and flailed like a bull rider on a good ride. Someone liked her music. She was gonna be the sweetheart of the rodeo someday.

"And one last flip." He got the spatula under the final pancake and air flipped it, managing not to hit the range hood.

Little Rosie squealed like she knew what he'd done. God, that was cute as fuck.

"Look at you, like a fancy short-order cook." Jim leaned past him to heat up syrup in the microwave, and they pressed together a moment.

His whole body tightened.

"Well, I'm a short everything, right, babe?"

Jim gave him a long, slow once-over, like he was measuring his fucking soul. "Not everything."

That was not helping the ache in his groin. "Well, now, that I'm glad you remember."

That laugh? That was everything—low and wicked, but also honestly tickled.

He filled plates with food. If Rosie was only three months, she wasn't old enough for solid food, so it was just the two of them. They could have a breakfast feast. "Here we go."

"It smells great. Thank you. I—Thank you."

"You're welcome, honey." He was glad Jim was choosing his words. He didn't want to fight. Austin was gonna figure this out. How to do this, whatever this was.

Jim dug in, eating like he was starving. Austin remembered that about Jim. The man was always busy, always working, always hungry.

He let himself eat the same way, maybe slower, but as much as he wanted. That bacon was like heaven. Damn.

They grinned at each other, for a moment in perfect accord, and he wanted to stay in that moment forever. Things would get hard and he knew it.

Good thing he was a bull rider. They knew how to be tough.

Chapter Six

"What the hell are you doing, Bubba?" John's voice damn near blew out his eardrum over the phone.

"Our bull broke his rental." Shit. He had been hoping for a little bit of respite from the family – a couple days, maybe.

"That's no excuse to sleep with him!"

His eyebrow shot up so fast, his cheek hurt. "Excuse me?" Not that it was John's business, but, "He slept in the office."

John grunted into the phone, the frustration getting to him. "Uh-huh. For how long?"

"Shut up." That wasn't up to John.

"Well, he has to have called someone about his truck."

He kept his voice measured. "He has."

"Good. You just... You said." John blew out a long breath. "You left him."

"Are you smoking?"

"What?"

Ha! He had John, just like always. He didn't have to even threaten to call Momma anymore. "Gotta go, man. Call me about the business insurance."

"Yeah. I will. I—"

"Bye." He hung up on John.

Jim had no idea what was going on, but dammit, he was curious, turned on, and he had guilt. That was the best he got.

Austin was surprising him at every turn. Cooking him breakfast. Helping him with chores. Sitting with him and Rosie and watching a movie. He felt like a long-tailed cat in a room full of rocking chairs, and he was buzzing—top to bottom.

It was partly a good buzz, but he knew it would end. And then he would feel bad for playing house when he knew it wasn't real. God help him.

"You look real serious, honey. Everything okay?" Austin came out from hanging his shirts in the laundry room. He'd done a load of laundry after they'd run out to grab the rest of Austin's stuff out of his rental. Of course, now Austin was wearing nothing but a pair of jeans, feet bare, chest bare.

Jesus Christmas.

"Dealing with the insurance." *Wanting to lick you all over, that's all.*

"Ah. That sucks. I would say I'm sorry, but I'm not too hurt since I get to stay and visit with you." Austin leaned past him to grab a coffee cup, and he almost exploded.

His hand reached out like it had a mind of its own, and cupped that teeny tiny heinie.

Austin's breath caught, and he straightened up to look at Jim head on. Inches away. "You want that, honey? You can have it."

"I've always wanted it." Stupid or not, logical or not—he'd always wanted it.

"That's good to hear. I want you too, but I ain't gonna push. Today."

They hadn't discussed how long Austin would stay, but it sure sounded like he didn't intend to go anywhere right now.

That was both wonderful and scary. He'd seen the schedule online. He knew Austin was off for almost two months. He didn't know if he could survive two months having Austin and then none. Worse, he didn't know if he could survive walking away again. "Fair enough. Want a beer?"

"Yessir. I would like that. You tell me when you want me to take the steaks out to make for supper."

"I never knew you liked to cook so much."

Austin chuckled. "We ate out, huh? It's been the last couple of years. I like being able to control what all goes in my food. I love road food. You know that. But all that salt and sugar…"

"Yeah… I can do basic stuff—biscuits, burgers, chicken on the grill, omelets, sausage."

"I've read a lot of cookbooks on my Kindle when I'm traveling. Dreaming of retirement."

He turned his head to stare. "Really? I've never heard you say that word before."

Austin's cheeks went dark. "I'm long in the tooth for a bull rider. And I've broken three bones this year."

Jim winced, but he was aware. "Yeah, I know. I swear I felt it when you broke your wrist on the gate." He knew how amazing Austin rode, but no one—no one—avoided injury.

Austin's gaze flashed to his again, something hungry there. "It hurt like a bitch. But the one that really got me was that damn rib. Every time I lifted my free arm…"

"Yeah…" He reached out, stroked his hand down along Austin's torso. "Is it better?"

"It is. Finally. I took off an event, and then we've been two weeks. I just need to stop stretching all that connective tissue."

The scar was right there under his fingers, new and still red and weird. He'd always been a little freaked out when Austin showed up with a new one.

"Well, let me know if you need anything." Was he still touching? He thought he was still touching.

"I will." Austin took his hand and pressed it flat, right over Austin's chest. He could feel Austin's heartbeat thudding.

He nodded, because yes, him too. So much. "I need...fuck, man. Please, I want to kiss you."

"Then come over here." Austin grabbed his arm, swinging him around like they were dancing, pulling him chest to chest and offering that damn fine mouth up like a gift. He bent and took the offer, needing too much for even a hint of class, a touch of control. Austin opened right up, hand sliding up behind his head to hold him there.

They might have been apart for what seemed like an age, but this much hadn't changed. The need they had for each other was like an explosion, like pouring gasoline on a fire. He grabbed Austin's ass and hauled him up, devouring the soft lips. They clung to each other, the kiss going deep, their tongues tangling. The heat went supernova when Austin circled his hips, rubbing.

"Come to the bedroom?" Rosie was sound asleep in her crib, and he had the baby monitor in there.

"Hell, yes." Austin took his hand, and there was no more letting him lead. This was the confident lover he knew so well, pulling him into his room and kissing him again.

Austin didn't waste a second—those clever fingers worked his buckle open, tearing off his belt. He sucked in, letting Austin pop the top button. Thank God the man was careful with his zipper because he was hard as a rock and it might have snagged painfully.

"Mmm...pretty baby." Austin shoved his briefs down and grabbed a hold of his cock, stroking him from base to tip.

"Austin!" His head fell back, his hips rocking. "Oh, damn. Damn."

"You been needing a touch, haven't you?"

He shook his head. Not a touch. Austin's touch.

"No?" Austin squeezed. "I been missing you, honey. So bad. I think you might have missed me some too."

"You. Jesus, I laid awake at night dreaming about you." He didn't know if he ought to make that confession, but his dick was in control.

"Oh, damn, baby." Austin worked his way up, which was maybe backward, to work off Jim's shirt. Then the jeans and boots came off, Austin kneeling in front of him to do the job. He hoped he knew what happened next, but he still swore like a sailor when Austin's lips touched the head of his cock.

He whimpered and reached down, fingers brushing through Austin's short hair as lightning shot up his shaft and settled in his balls.

Austin glanced up, those gray eyes dark with need, then slid right down on Jim's cock, sucking all the way. Down. Then up, tongue swirling around the head.

"Fuck. Fuck…" He couldn't help himself—either his words or the way his hips moved.

"Mmmhmmm." Austin's noise vibrated around him, and he moaned, balls pulling up.

"Gonna make me come, Austin. It's too soon."

Austin popped off his cock. "I know you're good for more than one, honey."

"I—yeah, I bet I am." He felt like he could come a thousand times.

"Then hush and let me make you feel good." Then Austin was back on him, licking and sucking, driving him out of his mind. Still, he took Austin's advice, letting himself melt back against the wall with a long sigh. Austin set about making him come, warm hands sliding up his thighs to push between his legs, one under his balls, one back behind so a finger could tap at his hole.

"Yes..." He would totally take Austin's cock, give the cowboy the ride of his life.

A soft chuckle was enough to make his belly go tight as a drum, a harsh sound escaping him.

"Austin!" He grabbed Austin's shoulder, his toes curling as he fought the urge to come. It was a lost cause, though. That finger pressed inside him and it was all over.

He shot so hard his brains rattled in his skull. For a long moment he couldn't breathe, his whole body seized up from the strength of his orgasm. His teeth chattered for a second, and then Austin moaned, the sound vibrating all along his shaft.

He tugged at Austin's hair, which was just long enough to get a bit of a grip. "Bed, cowboy."

"Mmhmm. Bed. I want you, Jim. I want to sink into your tight ass."

Said ass clenched right up, his muscles tight as anything. "God, yes. I got...well, I have some stuff, but the condoms might be old."

"They last three to five years, baby."

"Well, then." He'd bought them the last time he'd packed to go see Austin about a year ago. "You know when I used them last."

"Do I? I bought some a few months ago." Austin rose, leaning in when he stiffened. "Hope springs eternal, and I was still hoping you'd show up. I haven't used any except to keep the sheets clean in the fancy hotels."

"I remember that. I thought that was charming as hell."

Austin laughed, sounding a little breathless when Jim started on the buttons of his jeans. "Well, you know, the cheap hotels bleach the hell out of their sheets. The big places use OxiClean or whatever."

"Mmhmm..." He leaned down, kissing the curve of Austin's shoulder as he pushed the jeans open.

Austin's skin drew up with goosebumps. "You feel damn good."

"I need you... You up to letting me ride?" Jim never felt so sensual as when he was with Austin.

"I am. I like to watch you. You know that."

He flushed, but only because that brought to mind the time Austin had put him on his knees on the bed facing the dresser mirror across the way, letting them both watch as Austin fucked him. The memory made him sweat. "I do. I remember everything about us."

It had warmed his belly a lot over the last year.

"Good." Austin stripped out of his jeans and underwear. "I want you thinking about me as much as I do you. It's only fair." That hot cock bounced up, slapping Austin's belly.

He reached out and cupped the heavy balls, rolling them gently. "I thought a lot. All the fucking time."

"Uhn." Austin rocked up on his toes, then back down into his hand. "Let me..." He backed away to crawl on the bed. "Get the condoms and lube, baby. I'm rarin' to go."

Jim found himself chuckling, because this was why he'd fallen in love with Austin—the pure, simple need.

He grabbed the rubbers, finding the half-full bottle of lube.

Austin was slowly stroking himself when Jim got back, and his mouth went dry, his desire ratcheting right back up. He wanted that piece of rope so damn bad.

"How do you want me?" Jim asked.

"Wet and ready, baby. Gimme a show."

"Austin..." His cheeks heated, but the words woke him up, all over, and he propped one leg on the bed so he could slick himself up.

"That's it. Christ, you're gorgeous." Austin rocked up, dancing on the bed, fucking his own hand. "You look so decadent like that. Your lips are all swollen, your cock is stiff again."

Everyone on the circuit said his man was one of few words. Jim knew he was a poet. He hadn't ever needed anyone so bad. Never. He bent his head down, fingers moving faster, harder. He wanted to be riding in about eight seconds...

Jim huffed out a laugh, but Austin was grinning when he looked up, not mad.

"'M ready to ride, cowboy." He wanted to take every inch.

"Then come on, baby. Get over here and climb aboard." Austin held out a hand, wiggling those come-get-me fingers, which never failed to really get to him.

So he wiped off on a t-shirt tossed over a chair and grabbed Austin's hand, letting the man reel him in until he was right there, kneeling astride Austin's thighs so he could roll a condom down over his main prize. That was long and thick and so perfectly needy for him.

God, yeah.

"Uhn!" Austin arched up, under his hands as he smoothed the condom into place, muscles bunching and flexing.

"You still have the best abs I've ever seen."

Austin laughed, a little breathless. "All those crunches. Got to be able to sit up on a bull."

"Mmmhmm." He traced the ridged muscles with the fingers of one hand, feeling how smooth that skin was, how hot. "You know how many times I've screamed that at the TV? Sit up, Austin. Mind in the middle."

"Well, now it's your turn." Those gray eyes looked almost silvery, fever bright for him as Austin stared at him. Those strong hands settled on his hips, pulling him up and forward, dragging him over Austin's cock, which prodded his balls. "Now, Jim. I need you right now."

"Now." His chin tucked to his chest as he curled up, tilting his hips to put Austin's cock at his hole. The feeling of the broad head pushing into him made him moan, the pressure huge. It had been too damn long, and he'd missed this man inside him so much.

Jim sank down, biting his lower lip, but Austin reached up, popping it out of the grip of his teeth with his thumb. "That's mine, baby. You want someone to chew on it, you tell me."

He laughed, but it was full of strain, and he worked to get the last few inches in, tried to get his ass down on Austin's lap.

"Breathe."

His breath whooshed out of him, and Jim sucked another load in. "I was holding it."

"I know." Austin petted him, hands sliding over his belly and thighs, one stopping to stroke his cock for a few pulls. "So damn tight. So hot inside. So damn amazing. Jim, you gotta move soon. You have to. I can't take it."

"Move." He nodded furiously, his whole body shaking with need. The muscles in his thighs threatened to seize up, but he lifted, then lowered, feeling Austin inside him with every move.

There was no way his fingers could even come close to this. No toy. This was Austin. This was his damn lover, and they were in this together.

"More." Jim braced his hands on Austin's chest, bouncing up and down.

"Fuck! Jim. Yeah. Like that. Just like that." One hand landed on his hip, helping him, the other back on Jim's dick now, stroking him in time with their thrusts.

Oh, damn, they were cooking with gas, and he was going to lose it.

"More." That was all he could grind out, and he panted, his body rolling, rocking, the ride way smoother than Austin's usual wild and wooly moments on a bull.

"More," Austin agreed, bucking up, and there was the

break in the rhythm, the first sign that Austin was about to go off too.

They wheezed and grunted, sweat dripping. This was the best kind of hard work, and his muscles started to clench up, his body fighting with his will to make this last.

"Come for me, baby. Let me see it. Let it carry me with you."

That was all it took for him to go right over the edge. Jim shot so hard his teeth rattled, his body sawing back and forth as he came in great spurts over Austin's chest.

Austin froze, face set in a grimace Jim knew well, then he felt it as Austin started to spasm, his orgasm rolling through him in a way Jim could see as well as feel.

God in heaven, that was a beautiful man.

"Damn, baby. Damn."

"Uh-huh." He should be all suave and clean up, but he just slumped down on Austin's chest and tried to catch his breath.

Which was when Rosie's cry came through the baby monitor.

Austin chuckled. "Perfect timing."

"Uh-huh..." At least they'd both gotten off. He groaned and pushed himself up, all baby-headed. "Coming, baby girl!"

After he cleaned up and dressed and shit.

What he would never admit out loud was it had been totally worth it.

Chapter Seven

Austin wondered if Jim was going to ask him when he was fixin' to leave.

He held little Rosie while Jim exercised the horses, and that little girl just cooed and wiggled in his arms, just as happy as a pig in shit. He was fascinated by her little fingers and her tiny nose which really looked like something out of a cartoon. She was a hoot. Even when she spit up on him. He figured that was a lot less gross than what bulls threw at him in the arena.

Still, he had a new long-term rental pickup, even if he had nowhere to be, and he reckoned Jim was going to start making noises. So he needed to work on what he was going to say about why he was determined to stay a bit.

He didn't intend to fuck this up again. No way. "You hear me, little girl? I intend to stay with you and your daddy."

She bounced with him, giggling, when he two-stepped her around. Looked like she was totally down with his plan. She knew that he was a good guy.

"You know what you need, little girl? A puppy. Every

ranch baby needs to grow up with their first dog. I think we need a dog."

She blew bubbles at him. Austin took that as a yes. Little Rosie was pretty darned agreeable.

"I know. I know. Wait until you're a teenager."

He looked up as Jim rode up next to the porch, Sunny sleek and ebony between his thighs. "How's she doing?"

"We are having a ball." He kissed the top of her head. "Right, baby girl?"

She blew another bubble.

"She looks great. You're okay with her? I'm going to brush Sunny and get her walked out."

"I am fab, honey. We'll look for something to make for lunch." They'd had some vitamin D time. Now it was time to feed his man. He thought Jim kinda liked his cooking, and liked learning that he enjoyed it.

Anything he could do to make Jim want to keep him around. Because he was going to be a good partner. He was. Whatever that meant to Jim.

"Thanks, babe. I'll be in after a few." Jim's warm smile while he watched him and Rosie made Austin feel ten feet tall.

"Come on, baby girl. You and me. We got a date with some sammies or something." He'd made eggs and sausage and some frozen biscuits for breakfast, so lunch could be simple.

She jabbered at him, just telling him God knew what. He got her in her swing so he could make them food, and she never even paused. What a good girl. He had one cousin who would scream every time someone set his ass down. He guessed every baby was different, and this one knew she was desperately wanted and loved.

He hummed as he pulled out bread and turkey, cheese and mayo. Mustard for him since it had no calories to speak of, and he'd slice a tomato in lieu of the cheese. He splurged on some things, but a sandwich was fine without the fat.

Jim came in with a bunch of tomatoes in his hands. "Mmm...smells good. We're having a banner crop this year."

"Yeah? Cool. I'll wash some up and slice them." Some salt and pepper and red wine vinegar and he would eat them like chips.

"Works for me." Jim put them in a colander in the sink. "Are you...how long are you staying, Austin? What are we doing?"

"Well, I'd like to stay until the break is over. Then I'd like to go get my own damn truck and come back." That was pretty clear, right?

"Oh." Jim blinked at him, then he swallowed hard. The pause stretched out forever, and Austin felt his heart fall until Jim's smile bloomed. "You should bring some of your shirts."

"I will." He grinned, the relief almost crushing. "I've bought most of what I need for the next month or so, but then I'll have to get my stuff. If that's okay." He thought it was. He sure as shit wanted it to be.

"Do you want to—I mean, this is a commitment. I want you here. I want to be a family, but you need to want it too."

He paused, spreading mayo on bread for a moment, trying to find the words. This needed to be right. "I want you." He held up the knife when Jim would have interrupted. "I was all mad at you, man. I was. But I see you with her, and I get it. Like soul deep. I guess I'm a cowboy all the way. We pick someone we love more than anyone else and have babies."

Jim held his gaze. "We do. It's how we're made."

"It is." He set things aside, moving to put his hands on Jim's hips. "I'm—I ain't gonna lie. Part of it is that I don't want to lose you again. But me and Miss Rosie? We understand each other."

"She's like...a miracle. A little, perfect miracle."

"She's amazing." He took a soft kiss. "I know we got a lot to do. Talk about. All that shit." He glanced at Rosie. She got older he'd have to watch his mouth. "But I'm not thinking on giving up."

"Oh." Jim's eyes shimmered, and that smile blossomed, transforming the craggy face into something beautiful. "That's good to hear."

"Yeah?" He grinned back. "That *is* good to hear." That would do all he needed for now.

Jim leaned forward, kissing him, soft and sweet, like the big cowboy was making all sorts of promises.

Oh, he did like—

"Son, what are you doing?"

Jim rolled his eyes so far they damn near popped right out and stood. "Do you need new glasses, Momma?"

"Well, no. That's why I'm asking, son." Jim's momma stood at the back door staring at Jim and him. Jim's brother looked just like her.

"I'm kissing Austin. You want to meet him?"

One dark eyebrow winged right up. "If you're going to be kissing on him in front of my grandbaby, I reckon you ought, son."

"Well, she might as well see it. Austin, this is my momma, Elena Donoghue. Momma, Austin McPherson."

"The bull rider, no?"

"Yes, ma'am." He let go of Jim and went to offer his hand. "Pleasure to meet you."

"You're the one he was all hang-dog over. You gonna be good to him now?" Miz Donoghue was fierce, but her eyes were kind, and she shook his hand like she meant it.

"I am." He would do his dead-level best, and he met her gaze with all the truth he could muster.

"Good. Y'all want to come to supper tonight? I'm making enchiladas." A shopping bag landed on the counter. "I found Rosita some clothes and a baby doll."

"Thank you, Momma. And we would love that."

He grinned. "I love enchiladas. Thank you." He would have to meet the parents sometime, right? Better that than get shot when he was out riding fence or something.

"Excellent. Five thirty. I'll make apple fritters. We'll play cards." She went over and peered at Rosie. "She's out. I was going to take her for a while, but—"

"You can keep her tonight, if you want, Momma."

That smile just lit up the entire world. "I want. I'll take her to see your Aunt Belinda tomorrow morning and bring her home with burgers at lunchtime."

"Sounds amazing." Jim kissed her cheek. "She danced with Austin all morning."

"She likes to dance. She's a musical little one."

As if on cue, Rosie tooted, long and loud, cracking them all up.

"Well, I'll see you at between five and six." Jim's momma hugged Jim, patted his arm, and headed out.

"I should have asked her to stay for lunch," Austin murmured.

"She's a woman on a mission." Jim's laugh was merry. "She's nosy and needs something to tell the aunties tomorrow."

"Well, she'll have it now. Busting in on us while we were kissing." He grinned at Jim. That had gone well, all things considered.

"Yeah. John will be calling in short order to read me the riot act about evil bull riders." Jim didn't look worried.

"We can be, at that." He needed to make a few calls too, but nothing that couldn't wait.

"Yeah, but—that's part of the appeal. That rush. Makes a man want to grab a hold and ride." Butter wouldn't melt in his lover's mouth.

"Anytime, baby." He winked, but then he moved back around to making lunch. His belly was rumbling.

Jim got in the fridge and pulled out some veggies and ranch dip. "Better than chips, right?"

"They are." Dip he could control. Chips he could devour without thought.

"I remember." And how fucking hot was that? That Jim remembered, cared. Shopped for him.

He had to wander over after he put the last piece of bread in place and take another kiss from Jim. Had to.

Jim bent and moaned, licking his lips, the act sweet as sugar. "Damn, baby."

"Uh-huh. Love how you taste." He slid one hand up behind Jim's head to hold them together.

"You make me hungry." Jim's eyes searched his. "I missed you, every fucking day."

"You know I missed you, baby." And this was important. "Wasn't anyone else. Period."

"No? Me either. Never. I only wanted you."

"Then we're good." Would it be that easy? No. But it could start that easy.

And God help him, he'd keep it up too.

He had to. This was the biggest ride he'd tried yet.

Chapter Eight

He was packed. He was going to fly to Dallas and get his truck, go the event in Houston, and come home. To Jim. He'd get his new driver's license and his registration at the same time.

Shit, he didn't want to go.

Rosie was teething and thinking about trying to crawl maybe. Jim'd bought a load of mustangs for the back forty, plus another sixty head of cattle. Hell, they were having the time of their lives. He was learning to be a ranch cowboy all over again. He'd been riding fence and separating calves and going roping. This was a shock, this leaving.

Jim was being easy about it, but Rosie acted like she knew, fussing when he put her down, reaching for him.

"You about ready, cowboy?" Jim came up, hands sliding over his hips. "You get your sponsor shirt?"

"I did. I'm all packed." He chuckled. "Not ready at all. I got to get my mind in the middle when I get there." He'd been working out solid the last two weeks. His abs were in shape, and he'd dropped the five pounds he'd gained.

"You'll do it. I'll be watching and rooting for you. Rosie will hex the bulls if they're mean."

"She will. That baby girl loves me." He adored her too. It had taken no time at all for him to start thinking of her as theirs, not Jim's.

"She does. You're her best friend in all the world." Jim glanced at him. "You thought on what all you want her to call you?"

"I wanted to talk to you. And I don't know what she'll call your folks. I don't want to step on toes." He'd thought about it obsessively, but she wasn't old enough for it to be a huge issue yet, so he'd been mulling it over on his own for now.

"We'll talk about it when you get back."

"Yeah. Yeah, we will."

"I got some thoughts about that empty room off the sunroom too."

He raised an eyebrow. "You do?"

"Uh-huh. You'll see." Jim gave him a nudge-wink kind of look.

"So long as I'm not sleeping in there, baby, I don't care. I belong in your bed."

"You do." Jim kissed him. Hard. "I've always thought so. This has been like a dream. I'm a little scared to have you go."

"Hey, this is my chance to prove my word that I'm coming back with my sh-tuff." That was important. Jim needed to be able to depend on him.

"You need your shtuff. It's important. You need to come home."

"I do, baby. Living out of a duffle sucks enough on the road." Not that his shit had stayed in the bag after day four. It had been starched and pressed and hung in Jim's closet.

"Yeah. I hear you. Bring everything. We'll make room." Jim took a long, soft kiss. "And make the short go"

"I will. You watch." He wanted more of those kisses, but he had to go or he never would. "Love you, baby."

"I love you. Come home to me. I'll be watching."

He nodded, then clapped his hat on his head and grabbed his duffel.

It was time to go to work.

"Is he gone?" John stood on the front porch with a bag of burgers and fries.

"He's in Houston, brother. He's riding." And Austin was coming back with his truck and shit. And Jim was going to believe in it, dammit.

"Ah. Well, I brought supper." John looked...resigned.

"Come in." They had to work together. They were neighbors. They were brothers. They had to figure this out together. Austin was—special. Even if he was a bull rider. Even if he left every weekend.

"Thanks." John came inside, handing him the bags. "I'm worried about you."

"Why? He's coming to stay, John. He says he wants to make it work." And Jim wanted to believe Austin.

"Because he flat told you he didn't want to settle down. So now he wants to play house? Why?" John looked about as confused as a fuzzy caterpillar going backward.

He got it, the confusion, but him and Austin, they'd talked on it. "It's been a year, man. That's forever in bull riding. We both know that can't last forever."

"Yeah, okay, but do you want to be his retirement plan?"

Jim rolled his eyes. "He's a million-dollar cowboy three times over. He has good investments. Next."

"What if Rosie falls in love with him and he deserts her?"

"What if he falls in love with Rosie and doesn't?" he shot right back.

"What if he gets hurt, Jim?" That one was asked quietly, John's expression solemn. "Then what?"

"He'll get hurt. We both know that." Jim shrugged, because they were cowboys. Getting hurt was part of it. "What if I get hurt? We work huge critters. Shit happens. You got a damn broke arm. Again." The 'moron' was implied.

"It's less broken than ripped up and surged on, but you get that one." John took the burger he'd unwrapped and put on a plate with fries. "Mom likes him."

"What does Pop say?" Mom liked the idea of happily ever after.

"He's cautious, but he says he seems solid." Their dad was salt of the earth, so that was quite a statement coming from him. Jim was tickled as a pig in shit.

"Well, Rosie loves him, and I think she's a good judge of character."

"Rosie's four months old. She loves warm milk and sucking on rubber."

Jim's lips twisted as he fought to hold back his laughter. "But she hates Linda Krell and her boyfriend."

"True." John laughed. "But a blind fool would dislike them."

"Listen to you. You're not gonna convince me to not be happy or to not give him a chance to keep me that way." John might as well know it.

"Okay, but if he hurts you, I'm going to run him over with a loaded horse trailer."

Jim pondered that. "That's fair."

"Good deal. Can you squeeze me some ketchup on the plate? Those little packs."

"Ah, now we know why you brought lunch to me."

"No shit."

Jim stood and headed for the fridge. "I have some Whataburger spicy ketchup in the fridge. Want?"

"God, yes. You know I love Alma's Grill, but sometimes I miss the road food."

They laughed, and he heard Rosie on the baby monitor, so he got John set up, then went to change her and bring her out. The simple, habitual act soothed his nerves, which were jangling a little from John poking him.

"Look at my little Rosarita!" John beamed at her, and Rosie crowed and wriggled, happy to be utterly adored.

He handed her over. "So, you had your say now?"

"I have. I love you, bro. I want you to be happy. But I want him to be good to you too."

"I love you too, you giant, nosy ass." He went to grab a bottle for Rosie. He could feed her in her bouncy chair while he ate his burger.

He had an amazing family who loved him. They were just going to have to learn to love Austin too.

Chapter Ten

Austin grabbed the top rail, then bent down, doing a wide squat to warm up his quads and hip flexors. He rode his short-go bull after two more riders, so it was almost time for him to load up. Then he could hit the road, hopefully with a check, and head home.

His phone beeped, and he smiled as he saw Jim's text pop up. <Good ride, cowboy. Don't let go.>

<Never> He sent back.

"You look pretty happy for a guy who spent the last month and a half in New Mexico, man."

He grinned at Cody Manor, who was one of his best friends on the big tour. "You here to give me shit or pull my rope?"

"I have to choose, dude?" Cody gave him a shoulder bump. "Supper after. I want the deets."

"If you're willing to hit something on the edge of town." He wanted to get through traffic so he could head north, but he would have to stop and get something for sure.

"I'm headed the same way, so sounds good."

"Perfect." Now he needed to focus on this ride. The rest of the world had to stop and leave him to work.

Cody knew him well, so he backed off until the bull was loaded, and Austin climbed the rail, ready to drop his boots and knees on either side of the bull. The bull came up, and he scrambled up out of the way, keeping his head out of range of them horns.

"Damn! Buddy Clark, get your ass over here." Cody called someone in to help keep his head from connecting with Iron Heels's, and that went better.

Finally he got settled, and he nodded his head, huffing out his breath as he focused on keeping his arm up, his heels moving, and his mind in the middle.

He didn't let himself think. Not one time. He just went with muscle memory. After the score he could think about Jim.

The bull spun into his hand, and he fought the urge to fall into the well the bull was making with his body, correcting like a mad thing. Austin sat up, chin down, chest up. He knew this. He could ride this freaking bull.

Six.

Seven.

Come on, asshole! Don't let go!

Eight.

The buzzer rang, and for a wild second, he thought he wouldn't be able to let go.

Then Austin's hand popped open and he lunged to the side opposite the horns. Cody was whooping for him, and Hank Landry, one of the bullfighters, caught him almost midair and spun him toward the chutes.

"Go!"

He went, but Austin got up on the rail in time to turn and watch the replay on the big screen. Oh, he looked good. He was spurring and correcting and—

"Ninety-two point three! Austin MacPherson took the event."

Hell yeah. Austin pumped his arms, and as soon as the bull was out of the arena, he went back out to take his little victory boogie and to fist bump the bullfighters.

"Good ride, cowboy!" Hank was all smiles for him. "Good to have you back."

"Good to be here." But he was ready to go home.

"Way to go, buddy!" Cody slapped his vest. "Go get your check and we'll hit the road."

"That's a fine plan. Los Cucos out on 290 sound good? That gets us past the worst of 610."

"Works for me. I got to get home to my girl. I got myself a check, so I'm good to go."

"Excellent." He trotted out to grab his check, grin for the cameras, and ignore the interview. Austin grabbed his phone and headed to the locker room, calling Jim.

"Look at you! You rocked it! Ninety-two!" Jim sounded absolutely over the moon.

"Right? Not a bad weekend. Covered all four." He was on top of the world. "I'm heading out in a few, but Cody and I are gonna stop once we hit 290 and eat."

"Sounds good. You driving straight through or spending the night somewhere?"

"I'm gonna come on. I get too tired, I'll pull off at a truck stop and take twenty. I want to get home to y'all." Austin pulled off his uniform shirt. He needed to get incognito so he could slip out. He and Cody had both parked a ways away so they could go on foot and skip fighting the cab line.

"Well, if you need to sleep, you get a hotel, you know? We'll be here with bells on. I got chicken breasts for the grill tomorrow."

"Sounds good, baby. I got you all sorts of shit to try." He'd stopped at Buc-ee's.

"I can't wait. Love you. Have a good supper, huh? Rosie's ready to see you."

"Love you too, baby. I miss you both. See you soon."

They hung up, so he pulled off his shirt, then tugged on a long sleeve tee that would cover his tattoos, changed out his sponsor-brand jeans for wranglers, and put on his comfy driving boots.

Cody popped up beside him, looking twice as redneck as he did cowboy. "Ready?"

"Yessir."

"Good deal. Let's hit the road, I'm starving." Cody was a baby and could still eat like a teenager.

They headed out, ducking past fans easily and walking the eight blocks to their trucks, chatting easily. "See you at Cucos, man."

"Yep. You will tell all."

He would. In fact, he couldn't wait to rave about Jim and Rosie.

Austin had a family, and he was going home to them.

There was a first time for everything.

Chapter Eleven

Jim made himself go to bed, because dammit, Rosie needed him to be awake in the morning, but when Austin pulled up into the ranch at four in the morning, he was up and moving immediately.

He hit the on button on the coffee pot on the way out to the back porch, pulling on a t-shirt over his shorts.

Austin stepped out, then grabbed his duffle and pulled it over one shoulder. His stuff in the back was all tarped up, so Jim hoped that meant they could leave it until Austin'd slept.

"Hey, stranger. How you doing?" Jim took Austin's duffle as soon as he hit the porch, the scent of arena dust like some strange-assed drug—part danger, part home, part adrenaline. "Nice truck."

"Thanks. Hoo, I was nodding off. I'm glad I'm home."

I'm glad I'm home. Jesus Christ, had there ever been such beautiful words? "Me too, man."

"Mmm. C'mere and kiss me. I got all sorts of crap in my duffle that couldn't stay in the truck. The rest can wait." Austin reeled him in to press their mouths together.

He wrapped one hand around the back of Austin's neck,

holding on, diving into that sweet, hungry mouth. They had to break for air a bit later, and they both gasped, just grinning at each other.

"I made coffee." He rested their foreheads together. "God, you taste good."

"Yeah? We could have pancakes. I'm starving. I can sleep after we do chores. You can have a nap with me when Rosie does." Austin was real good at scheduling sleep.

"I've got fresh pecans. Sit. I'll cook." He knew Austin had to be pooped.

"Yeah? I'll just have some coffee." Austin grabbed the pot, which had finished running, then poured them both a cup. Austin fixed them both up, setting Jim's on the counter before leaning back on the wall on the other side of the kitchen.

Someone had been sitting too long.

"You hit any weather on the drive?" He got out eggs and milk, butter and Bisquick. The normal act settled his soul, which was spinning, in shock that Austin'd come back for real.

"Not really. Almost got hit by a dust devil over by Conchas, but that was the worst of it. Sucker was huge." Austin made a spiral motion with his hand.

"It's been a wild year for it. That short-go ride was one for the books. You were spurring like a son of a bitch." He was so fucking proud of Austin that he couldn't hardly bear it.

"I looked like I knew what I was doing, huh? Cody says hey. He's angling for a visit, but I told him I need us time for a bit. Maybe in the spring." Austin chuckled and shook his head. "His girl is having a baby, and he's a little freaked."

"I can understand that. It's a wild time." He'd been terrified—about Rosie coming, about Modette changing her mind, about something being wrong with the baby, about whether or not he was an idiot.

"Yeah, I reckon so." Austin watched him, looking hungry.

His cheeks started to burn, but it was from pleasure, not embarrassment, and damn but he could take that.

"Mmmm. You look so good, baby." Austin's grin was just wicked.

"I look like I just woke up, and I'm in a Captain America t-shirt." He chopped up some pecans and threw them in, going for suave.

"Yep. It's a fine thing. I did an event, left the arena without a shower, and I've been on the road for a whole day. I bet I smell like cow poop and sweat." Austin chortled.

"Mmm...eau de cowboy." He glanced at Austin, and they both cracked up, tickled as all get out.

"So what did I miss? How many of your family came to yell at you?" Austin asked, moving finally to pull out syrup and butter and all.

"Only John, but we worked it out, and I got a burger out of it."

"Well, if you have to take a beating, at least get food. I got enchiladas verdes for mine."

"Cody give you hell?"

"Just cautionary tales of you ghosting me."

"I deserve it." He wasn't strong enough to break up with Austin, and it had felt like maybe they hadn't had a thing to begin with, if he was honest.

"Well, no more of that, huh?" Austin gave him another peck on the way by.

"No. No, we're going to make this work, and fuck the doubters."

"Now you're talking. Say I won't." That glinting grin warmed him. "Though I'd rather fuck you."

"After your pancakes and a shower." His lips twisted. "Maybe during a shower."

"Now that would be nice. You do got that seat in there."

"Mmhmm. I have a fancy-assed bathroom."

"I love it. It's got all the bells and whistles." Austin shrugged. "I might have to spring for a hot tub. Just to contribute."

"Oh man. I've been looking at those. I'm considering a pool and hot tub combo. Rosie's gonna love the water."

"You think so? A nice deck system with a gate. Make it safe for babies and dogs." Austin glanced sideways at him.

"I think that's a good idea. Don't want anyone getting hurt." Someone wanted a dog.

"Nope. Never." Austin finally sat, watching him, the look hot enough to cook those pancakes without the stove.

"So, you got a dog in mind?" He put the butter in the pan and started frying the pancakes.

"Well, I was thinking something ranch dog. Border collie would be better than a heeler or such. Less likely to nip. But I also like hounds. They're good with kids." Austin drew patterns on the table. He'd really thought on this.

"You find one that you like, and we'll get it. Maybe we ought to get two, so they can play."

"Maybe. I'll start with the shelters and rescues. I got a buddy who's a dog trainer."

He kind of felt like Austin had a buddy for every situation. That wasn't bad, not at all. It just amused him. Austin and his brother really had a lot in common.

He had always been more of a homebody. He couldn't help it. He loved to go, but he loved coming home even more. The ranch was his domain; the road was John's.

"Sounds good." Jim slid that last pancake on the plate, along with the microwave sausage he'd heated up. His momma would disapprove, but he hadn't felt like waiting for it to fry. "Dig in."

"I love your pancakes, Jim. They're worth every calorie." That was damn high praise.

"Thank you, sir." He took a bow. "I kinda like them too."

He knew not everyone fried them like he did, but this was how his momma made them, so it was how he did. A little butter did wonders.

"Mmm." Austin licked his fork. "That is some good stuff."

He stared. Even his sluggish four a.m. brain and body wanted to get some of that. "Eat your damn pancakes, cowboy. I have a shower and lube calling our name."

"I'm on it." Austin hooted, and Jim prayed his baby girl stayed asleep.

He had an itch that needed scratching. Bad.

Austin was home with a truckful of his shit. This was big. This was moving in together.

"You ready to celebrate, baby?" Austin stood, taking his plate to the sink.

"Yessir. I'll do dishes when Rosie-Posie wakes up. Let's go welcome you home." He dropped his dishes off and took Austin's hand. "I'm ready to play."

They had plenty of time to do work later.

Chapter Twelve

Austin and Jim settled into a pretty fine pattern. During the week, he was home, helping out on the ranch, eating supper with Jim's family, loving on Jim and Rosie. On the weekends, he headed off to events and made his pennies, and he had a good shot at the finals coming up. He was in the top three in the world right now and riding high.

Jim never gave him any shit about going, but Rosie? Rosie was beginning to pout at him, refuse to let him hold her every Sunday night. She wanted his happy ass home. He was her cowboy, and there was no denying that one bit.

He grabbed his duffle, putting it out on the bed. He would pack and try to sneak it out to the truck after they put her down for the night.

"You heading back out tonight or tomorrow?" Jim asked, leaning in the doorway.

"I'll take the redeye tonight." That way he could sleep all morning at the hotel. "East coast events suck."

"Yeah. Thank goodness the farthest we drive out is California with the bulls. You just parking at the Sunport?"

"Yeah. Long term is pretty cheap." He shook his head, still marveling at that. Dallas was a killer for fees.

"Cool. You like this event pretty well?"

"It's not my favorite." He grimaced. "It's cold up there by this time of year, and the hotel folks are polite but the food is... um."

"Bland?"

"Hoo yeah."

"Well, you have to make it through the finals, and then you can have all the enchilada casserole you want."

"I can." His belly rumbled. Austin got spoiled living with Jim. When he'd been on his own, it had been easy to eat a piece of fish and a stalk of broccoli. And Jim bought healthy as hell food most of the time. But damn, the Mexican food was so good. Even better were the breakfasts. Once little bit could eat, he foresaw a ton of long, lazy, post-chore breakfasts for them.

Brunch, really. Lord, he would give up all his calories the rest of the day to get brunch with Jim.

He packed jeans and socks, unders and t-shirts. His shirts could go in a garment bag.

"You better come love on your girl. You know she won't talk to you again 'til Tuesday."

"I know. I'm sorry, love. At least you're talking to me." He turned to grab Jim and reel him in.

"You have to work. I know it. I wish your shoulder was feeling better, though. Almost finals."

"Yeah." Austin fought not to roll his sore shoulder in response. It was on his free arm, and it had come right out two events ago. No bueno. But he had to make it through the season. Just two events left and then finals. He hated being hurt, but it was happening more and more often. "Gettin' old."

"Happens to the best of us, right?" Jim winked at him,

playing hard. "We'll have to make a rancher out of you, Mr. Papa."

"We will." Papa. God, that should scare him. It made him dizzy with happiness. He looped an arm around Jim, steering him out to see Rosie.

Rosie squealed when she saw him, opening and closing her hands in a little wave.

"Hey, baby! Look how pretty you are all in pink."

"You got time to eat with us?" Jim asked.

"Always." He managed his flights so he could get the most time with his man and baby. He would drive down to Burque and fly out about eleven p.m.

"Come on, baby girl. Let's go eat with Papa hmm?" Jim scooped her up, and she reached for Austin immediately. "Oh, I see how you are!"

Austin grabbed her in his arms and buzzed a kiss to her cheek. "Carrots tonight, bright one?"

She jabbered and cooed, telling him all about it. They were up to applesauce and carrots. She got about one mouthful for every ten spoonfuls they fed her.

"Good deal. I bet I get breakfast for supper." Jim would spoil him before he hit the road with an egg white omelet loaded with veg along with some whole grain toast.

"You can have biscuits and gravy, pancakes, or migas. Your choice."

"Damn. Migas, please." That was better than an omelet by far.

"Heavy on the salsa, light on the cheese?" Jim teased, but the man knew him. Hell, he'd called Austin's sister and learned how to make his stepmom's salsa. That was love.

"You know it." He got little bit in her baby chair and went to grab the tiniest bottle of carrots in history.

This was more fun than anything—watching her learn everything. He would never admit it to the non-dads on tour, but this was better than riding. He didn't get how some of the guys with a couple of kids didn't just stay home. Then again, most of them needed the money. Still, it was hard to leave Rosie. Leaving more than that had to be hell on earth. Shit, Ryder had six. Six little eyes asking him to stay. Damn.

"I tell you John asked me to go in on that new bull? J4-98?" Austin mentioned as casually as he could.

"Did he?" Jim's smile just bloomed. "What are you thinking?"

"I think it would be a good investment, but I wanted your input. If you don't want to go in with him, I don't want to step in it."

"John's got a knack for the buckers. Me? I'm better with the horses and the breeding programs, but John's got a nose for the bulls."

"Cool. Then we'll go with it." Austin beamed at Jim, tickled as a pig in shit. He wanted to contribute, and he could stand to invest in some diverse stuff.

Rosie slapped her hands on the tray, demanding his attention.

"Well, okay then, Miss Apples and Carrots. Let's do this." Austin never denied her when she was hungry. She was growing fast. She had a tooth now, and she could sit up on her own. It was amazing. Hell, he really had a hard time denying her anything he loved her so much.

"I love how you look at her," Jim said.

"She's special. She's ours." He said the words, and then held his breath, waiting for a reaction.

"She is," Jim agreed. "She's going to have you wrapped around her little finger. By the time she's a teenager, I bet I'll be the bad cop."

"I'll be the one tackling boys and making her holler, though." He loved that, the thought of long term.

"Yessir. You're way more likely to get physical." Jim gave him a glinting grin. "I'll just shoot 'em."

"Mean old daddy man," he teased.

"That's me. I'm the old bastard."

"I love it." He loved Jim more and more every day. Austin knew how lucky he was; Jim could have told him to fuck off. Hell, they'd damn near lost this thing they had together.

Now they had it back, and Austin was holding on tighter than he would his bull rope.

The scent of onions and peppers sauteed hit his nose, and for a second, he almost just said he was staying home, but he only had a few more rides.

If he could win enough between this event and the finals, he could start the next season with enough of a bye that if he needed surgery, he could have it.

He sighed, and Rosie blew applesauce bubbles at him.

"Hey, you can stay home."

"I was just thinking that. But I've got some momentum. And I have a sponsor event."

"Well, just so that you know you're welcome here. This is your home."

"Thank you, baby. It's starting to feel like it." His clothes in the closet. His boots and flip-flops by the door. His hats hanging on the hat rack by the kitchen door.

Even his framed picture of him and Ty Murray was hanging in the bedroom.

"I want it to be so you come back every time."

"I never want to live out of a suitcase again. This is it." That was serious as a heart attack.

"Good deal. Migas are almost done." Jim looked over his shoulders. "How's she doing?"

"Almost there, daddy man. She's eating to grow."

"It's hard work, learning how to sit up."

"It is. She wants to ride horses." Austin winked, and Jim just laughed.

"Probably."

He wiped her up, carefully taking off her bib, proud that she was pretty clean. The first few times he'd fed her had been a disaster. Hell, it hadn't gone easier for Jim. She'd only been at it for two weeks.

He grinned at her, and she gurgled, but no carrots came up. Yay.

Spectacular.

"You going to forgive me for leaving this time, girlie? I'm going to make us some bull money."

She blew a raspberry at him.

"I know. I do." He winked at her, and she giggled madly.

"She'll forgive you. You're her Papa."

"I am." He bent to kiss her, then tossed a towel over his shoulder in case she burped anything up and took her to sit at his spot at the table. She loved to sit with him when he ate. He wasn't sure if she was watching or loving her cuddles. Either way, what bliss. She was a snuggle bug.

Jim hummed, sliding food onto plates, then setting them on the table. He looked so damn hot in just a t-shirt and jeans.

"You want me to take her?"

"I got her. You'll have her all weekend." He winked, feeling a little *grr* again that he was leaving. He would have to ponder this feeling. It was pretty new. Jim would let him stay, no question. Hell, he'd probably enjoy it, so this was all on him. He'd have to talk to a couple of the older guys, see if this was like...what they were feeling when they talked retirement. If he won enough...

Shit. That was a long way away. He needed to focus on this weekend and get the job done.

After the Finals, he could start thinking about next year.

Not before.

Chapter Thirteen

Jim watched Austin get trampled, wincing at the way he was holding his arm. "Dammit!" he snapped, startling Rosie and making her cry. "Oh, shit. Shh...shh...Austin's just hurting. I can tell. We'll call him in a second."

Austin hated nothing more than sitting in sports medicine with an ice pack on, and that was where he was going to end up. Jim would chat with him, keep him busy. Maybe that would keep him from being all grumpy.

He texted with <let me know when I can call>, and then settled in his recliner, rocking Rosie, who kept looking for Austin, then dozing off again.

Bless her heart. It would take ages for her to understand where he went when he left her. She just knew he was gone.

His phone rang about ten minutes later, almost sending him jumping out of his skin, which would have pissed him right off, since Rosie was out like a light. "Whoa. Hey."

"Hey, babe. Sorry. Brady had to find my phone for me."

"How's the shoulder? Hanging in there?" *Won't you just come home, please?*

"By a thread, I reckon. It's hurtin' pretty good. Doc is probably going to give it a shot."

"Dammit." He wanted Austin home. They could let it rest, surg on it if they needed to, but it wasn't going to just hold. He knew it. He also knew Austin was a stubborn son of a bitch that loved to ride, so...

"It'll be done soon, babe. I'll get it fixed in the off-season."

"I know. I do. You can do it in town." And then go and tear it up again.

"Yeah. Ow. Damn it, Dane!"

Jim bit back a grin. He'd had supper with Dane Meechum and his wife. Man was a damn fine medic but had no bedside manner.

"Just baby it, won't you? It's wanting to pop." And he hated knowing that.

"I know. I'm not getting any younger, huh?" Austin grunted. "Miss you and our girl."

"We miss you. She's sleeping hard right now, dreaming of unicorns and ponies." He wanted to tell Austin to come home. They could make a life together here at the ranch.

"Yeah. She's something else, that baby girl. Huh? You should see her, Dane. She's getting big."

He could hear Dane ask for pictures, and everything got a little distant as Austin showed her off. She'd changed a ton in three months.

They all had.

Jim was used to having another adult to talk to, to having someone to share his life with, his bed with. Hell, he was used to sitting and playing goofy-assed video games in the quiet part of the evening. And the loving was none too shabby.

"Damn. Now I'm all cold sweat. I want to come home."

"So come on early. I'll have John drive me to the Sunport so I can drive you home one way or the other." Momma would watch Rosie.

"Yeah? I didn't make the short go anyway." That was a little growly. But then Austin's voice picked up some humor. "Doc says I wouldn't have been able to do it if I want to do the finals in two weeks. I'll get an earlier flight as soon as he lets me go."

"Sounds good. I'll get Momma to watch Rosie tonight. Text me with your flight details, and I'll pick you up." He just needed to make a few phone calls. Easy-peasy.

"Will do, babe. Lord, what a damn event." Yeah, Austin had told him about a crazed fan at the signing Friday too.

"I'll talk to you in a few, babe. Love you." Austin was coming home.

"Love you too. Ow. Bye." Austin hung up, and he started calling people.

Momma. John. His foreman, Christian.

Time to rescue his roughstock rider from the airport.

"Okay, I want you to keep immobilized and—" Doc cut off when two riders came hurrying in, another rider draped over their shoulders, his feet dragging. Not just another rider, the number two in the world, Cristiano Morao.

"Shit, what happened?" He was up and moving to help without a thought.

"Horn to the head. Scattered his chickens." Jimmie Davies shook his head. "It was fucked up, man."

"Damn it." He hated to see a man down. Cris had been riding so well.

"Get back up in the bed, MacPherson," Doc snapped.

"Doc, Austin's made the short go now. He's got to get ready to ride."

Austin blinked. "I have?"

"You got an eighty-three. That's enough to move you up now that Cris is out."

"Shit."

"MacPherson, that shoulder needs rest."

"I know, but—" It was one ride. Just one. He needed the points. "But you're gonna have to tape me up good, Doc. I ain't gonna miss this."

He'd have to call Jim back, and he sent up a prayer his man didn't get mad.

"Are you sure, son? You pop it, the finals are out."

"I know. But I don't do it, I end up with a lower spot going in. Then I have to ride way more bulls in four days. Boom, boom, boom." Another event win and he might only have to cover two bulls for the whole finals even. Depended on Cris.

"It's up to you, but I don't recommend it."

"I hear you." He just didn't care. He needed this ride. He grabbed his gear and headed to get his vest on.

First though, he called Jim. "Hey, babe."

"Hey, you. You get a better flight? Momma's already picked Rosie up."

"I didn't. One guy fell out, so I'm in the short go. I get this ride, I can take it easy at the finals in two weeks." He held his breath, waiting to see if he got his ass handed to him.

"What about the shoulder? Is it strong enough?"

"Doc says no, but it's my free arm. I just had him tape it up. It's not like I got to hold on with it. I just have to keep it up enough not to smack the bull."

There was a moment of silence. "Well...are you sure, cowboy? I mean, I'll come pick you up at the airport regardless, but...you know you don't have to, right?"

"I know." He did know. "I just—I need to do this. I got ideas about backing off next season, but I got to hit well on this one to do it. I—it's important, Jim."

"Okay. Okay, I hear you. I—I want you to know that this is your place too, though, okay? That you have a real home. Here."

"I believe that. I do. I got to contribute though. I do." Did that make sense? He wasn't going to be the rodeo trash who mooched off his lover. That was what people would say.

"You do. I want—we can make it official, you and me." Jim sounded so weird.

"We can what?" He wasn't sure he understood. Then it dawned on him. "Oh, honey. We need to talk, but I'm not sure now is the time." He needed to be face to face to have that discussion.

"I—sure. Good ride, cowboy. Don't get hurt. I'll pick you up at the airport tonight." The phone went dead.

"Shit." He had a feeling Jim had misunderstood him. He was about to push the button to call back when Cody came trotting up. "You're up second, man. I need your rope."

"Coming." He needed to look at his draw and get ready to ride.

Whatever Jim thought, his lover was coming to pick him up, so he'd get to explain. That was the important part.

He grabbed his rope and his helmet and headed out, his shoulder throbbing. He could do this. Then he was gonna go home and pour his heart out.

First, though, he was going to ride this fucking bull into the dirt.

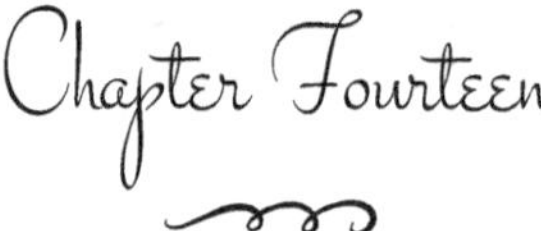

Chapter Fourteen

J im stood in his front room, watching the short go, telling himself he wasn't mad.

They'd only been back together less than six months. Of course Austin wanted to take a little time. It was totally logical to give themselves time. Austin was so right.

He took a deep breath, trying not to pace. Austin was up soon. Then he would go grab a bite to eat on the road somewhere to kill enough time before he went to get Austin. His mom had Rosie, the feeding was taken care of. So he should take advantage of being able to eat his weight in something decadent.

The first rider went up and down so fast he missed it and needed to watch the replay to see it. Damn.

The bulls had been on fire all afternoon from what he'd seen. He'd missed some while he was making calls. He hadn't known Cristiano had gotten hurt.

Then he saw Austin, with Cody and Hank pulling his rope. Austin looked pale, but his lips were tight and determined.

"Okay, cowboy. You ride that son of a bitch."

He stood there, holding his breath, his hands clenched. Austin got up on his rope, hand in the rigging, then nodded his head. The gate flew open, the bull going around to his right, which had to put Austin in the damn crunch. Jesus that had to hurt.

Austin was smack down in the middle, looking forward, and things looked solid. Austin made the eight, and Jim hooted, applauding hard.

"All right! Come on, you asshole. Get off."

The bull broke the other way at the last second, and with his free arm half taped down, Austin couldn't recover. Jim watched, eyes wide, as Austin went down in the well and the bullfighters sprang in to try to keep the bull's head up and keep Austin from getting hung up in the rope.

He saw the way the bull bucked, snapping that riding arm taut, and Austin's head flew back, eyes rolled back in his head. "Get him off!" he screamed. "You get him out of that rope now!"

John walked in the front door. "What the fuck? I'm here to run you... Oh, Jesus fucking Christ."

Jim was fixing to throw himself at the TV and shake it when Austin popped free, he and one of the bullfighters going off like helicopter blades. They went down hard, and it didn't take a genius to see that Austin's free arm was at an angle not found in the human body when it was whole.

"I need a flight," he snapped. He was going to have to pack a bag.

"On it."

His eyes were still on the television. *Come on. Come on. Get up. Please. Please, get up.*

Austin didn't though, for the longest time, then they hauled him up and dragged him out.

Fuck.

John was clicking shit on his phone. "Find out who his flight is with, and I'll call them."

"It's in my email." John has access to his Gmail since he used the Google calendar for scheduling. "I'm going to pack."

"Okay. I'll let Momma know she'll have Rosie a few days."

"Thanks." Goddamn it. Okay. Phone. Charger. Shirts. Jeans. Jacket. Briefs. Socks. Ditty bag. Done.

"You know this is crazy, right? He's an adrenaline junkie."

"Not now. John. You know the rodeo as well as I do. I can't ask him to change, and I love him."

"But you have a baby."

He slammed his hand against the wall. "Sixty percent of rodeo guys have babies! I'm not an idiot. Just trust me. For once, just believe in me?" He needed his family's support, and he needed to know they had his back.

John stared at him for a long moment, then nodded. "Okay. Okay, bro. I'll trust you." John's fingers flew. "Got you a flight. We need to get moving."

"Let's go. I'm ready. I'll call Momma from the road."

"Yeah, I talked to her, but you'll need to chat with her and make sure it's all good."

"I will." He clapped John on the shoulder. "Thanks. I can't just not go."

Austin needed him and, if he was honest, he needed Austin. They really did have to talk.

Jim grabbed his bag. "Let's hasta."

Chapter Fifteen

Austin woke up in the hospital. He knew it because the bed was impossibly uncomfortable, and the place smelled like antiseptic. What he didn't remember was how he'd gotten there.

His free arm was in a brace, his left wrist was in a cast, and he felt like hammered shit. "Oh fuck."

"Hey, cowboy. You're awake."

That tired voice was familiar and unexpected as hell, and he tried to focus. "Jim?"

"Yep. Very good. You need anything?"

"I—" He swallowed hard, his dry throat making a loud click. "Water?"

"Right here." Jim stood and brought the straw to his lips, the cold water just what he needed.

"Oh. Good." He took in a little more. "How bad is it?" It wasn't if you got hurt in bull riding. It was when.

"Broken wrist, broken collarbone, they totally rebuilt your shoulder joint. It was destroyed."

"Jesus." Well. No finals for him. Maybe no season next year. "You sign off on it?"

"Yes. I didn't know you'd switched me to medical power, honey."

"We're together, baby." He tried to move, but nothing was working. "An us. I knew you'd be here and would be level-headed with Doc."

Jim sat where Austin could see him easy. "It had to be done. You'll need that shoulder to hold Rosie."

"I will." Austin wasn't mad. Well, maybe at himself. He could have been home right now. "I feel pretty stupid."

"You're a bull rider, honey. They only come in pretty and stupid." Jim winked at him, eyebrows gyrating madly.

"Listen to you. Where's our girl?" He missed her sweet face.

"Staying with her *abue* for a couple of days until I get you home."

"Probably best. Her poor baby ears aren't up to flying." Lord, this bed. It sucked. His butt hurt in places backends weren't supposed to.

"No. Flying's going to suck for you, too, but not as much as driving home from here." Jim kissed his temple, the touch warm and dry, like a summer afternoon at the ranch. "They're saying you'll go home tomorrow, and I thought we'd take one day in a hotel, and then fly home the next day."

"Yeah. Yeah, that sounds good, baby. I swear, is this an emergency room bed?"

"No. But the nurse said shit would be uncomfortable and as soon as you woke up I could use these extra pillows to help you prop up." Jim grabbed some pillows and started jostling and arranging and shit.

"You're an angel."

Jim was padding him with something close to glee, pushing the pillows under his shoulder, under his knees. "Hardly."

"Mmm. Feels like it to me. You wanting to yell?"

"Yell? About what?" Jim actually looked confused.

"Me riding? Cutting you off when you called? I was thinking you got my answer wrong, baby." He was hurting bad, but Jim needed to know this.

Jim met his gaze, eyes serious as a heart attack. "You're a bull rider. You ride when you shouldn't. And I get it. We haven't lived together long. When you're ready, I'll be waiting."

"Hey." He tried to sit up. "No. No, that wasn't it at all." He gagged, nausea like to kill him.

"Love. Love, breathe." Jim grabbed the pitcher and helped him get a cold drink, which settled him immediately. "There you go. You just got surged on. You have to relax."

"Sorry. This is important. I meant I wanted to wait to see you, to have that conversation face-to-face."

Jim nodded, kissed his forehead. "I'm right here."

"I know. I do. I want that with you, Jim. I want forever." And he wanted Jim to understand.

"I want to marry you, raise Rosie, run the ranch. I want to be a family, you and me." Jim never looked away, never blinked. "I love you. You're it for me."

Austin felt like he might explode, but this time in a good way. "I want that too. I was always gonna say yes, baby. Always. You and Rosie are it for me too. I mean it. Y'all are my friggin' soul, Jim."

"Then we'll do it. We'll get married. Right now, I want you to heal." Jim kissed him real soft, and it felt like a promise, like they'd just set their vows before the good Lord Himself. "If you'd have said no, you would still have a home with us. I need you to know that."

"I do." He believed it in his soul. Jim was solid as a rock when he'd made up his mind. "You're my cowboy."

"Yessir. Balls to bones." Jim cupped his jaw. "Now, lean

into the pillows and rest. I'll find us something horrifying to watch together."

"Thank you." He was engaged. Jesus, he needed to get a ring.

His thoughts whirled, but Austin was hurt and freaking tired, and as soon as he sat back and let the pillows take his weight, he was out like a damn light.

Chapter Sixteen

J im pinched the bridge of his nose between his finger and thumb, telling the damn headache to back the fuck off. "They're releasing him today, and then we'll get on a flight tomorrow. There's a hotel right here that's used to dealing with patients."

"But he's okay, mi'jo? He's going to be whole?" Momma sounded worried as hell, but Jim had seen Austin way lower.

"He just needs to heal, Momma."

"And the bulls?" He loved how she said 'bools'. Loved it.

"Not this year. The doctor says probably no more rodeo."

"Ah. That happens. Bulls are big and mean." She paused. "He won, huh? I saw that. The event."

"He did." Austin had ridden for a damn ninety, and had taken a thirty-thousand-dollar check for it. And a bonus from the event sponsor, who was one of Austin's sponsors too. Team Bullet Jeans.

"Good. It's good to go out on top."

"You're right, Momma. Is Rosie okay?" He'd already asked, but he'd ask over and over again.

"She's fussing over missing you, but John got some more

of her things, and she's happy enough. She'll be all over you when you come home, huh?"

"Day after tomorrow, I'll be there. I swear." He sighed softly. "I really appreciate your help."

"I'm just glad Austin is coming home with you and isn't in the hospital for weeks, you know? You just take your time."

"Thanks, Momma. I'll email with info." Jim hung up with her, and grabbed himself a Coke and a packet of cheese crackers. Supper of champions.

He took a deep breath. Lord, he was tired, he missed his desert and his ranch, and his heart ached for Rosie, but he knew Austin was hurting and a little wigged out about how his season had ended. So he needed to be zen.

The doctor was in the room when he walked back in, and he nodded at her. "Hey, Doctor."

"Hello. I was just explaining to Mr. MacPherson that his shoulder was in trouble. Serious trouble. He needs at least six months of therapy, and no more riding on the bulls."

"Ah." Dammit. He'd wanted to be in here for his particular conversation.

Austin gave him an unreadable look, and the words, when they came, were dry as caliche dust. "Yeah. Looks like I need to talk to John about investing sooner rather than later."

"He's ready to work with you, no problem." He didn't want to be the bad guy, that wasn't his job—to tell Austin what he was or wasn't going to do with his body.

"Well. I will help coordinate with the therapy in… I believe the closest place to you is Santa Fe."

"Possibly Albuquerque," he said. "But my mamaw went to get her rehab with her hip replacement in Las Vegas." He paused, remembering they weren't in New Mexico where they belonged. "I mean the one in New Mexico. Not Nevada."

"Oh? Oh, I see. Yes, perfect. I will put these in his release orders."

"Thank you." He smiled at the doctor, and Austin nodded.

"Yep. I'm on it." Austin didn't sound totally with it, if he was honest.

Jim waited for the doctor to leave, and then he went to sit, propping himself on the bed on one butt cheek. "You okay?"

"Well, I reckon I have to be." Austin chuckled, and that eased him some. That wasn't a fake laugh. "Doc called from the tour before this guy came in. He'd already consulted and come to the same conclusion." Austin tried to shrug, he thought, and grimaced. "Ow. Anyway, he says if I want to risk losing the use of my arm every time I ride, go for it. I won't do that to us and Rosie."

"No one rides forever, right, cowboy? You have a ranch and a family to take care of." Jim knew this was hard, but he was happy that Austin was willing to come home.

"Yep. I expected to have a few more years, but I went out with a bang." This time Austin's chuckle was a little rough around the edges, and plumb raw in the center. "When can we go home?"

"I got us a hotel room for tonight, and a first-class flight out tomorrow morning. We'll be home by supper tomorrow." He needed to see his baby girl.

"Whew. Look at you, springing me." Austin beamed, and the expression was for real then. "I want to be home to recover. I'll only be totally worthless until the wrist heals. Then at least half of me will work."

"You can help with Rosie, invest with John, be home and enjoy her first Halloween, her first Christmas." The important things.

"Her first..." Austin blinked hard, then whooped, shocking the living fuck out of him. "I feel like Scrooge on Christmas. I didn't miss it!"

"You didn't. You get to be there for her firsts, Papa." Jim's heart felt like it was filled with butterflies. "Shit, if I'd've been a bird, I'd have hit the window."

"I will be there, with bells on." Those bright eyes glinted at him. "That makes a lot of things better, baby. That's all right."

"I'm tickled as a pig in shit to hear that." Jim squeezed Austin's toes. "Once they get the IV out, I got some big, cheap sweatpants and some jeans and slip-on shoes for you."

"Good deal. Can I have a shower tonight?"

"Nope. But I can give you a sponge bath. They want me to wait until you're not in a hotel for the shower. Just in case. Momma is going to get Aunt Bobbi in to clean our bathroom and Lord knows we already got us a seat in the shower."

Austin didn't need anyone but him to help with washing.

"A sponge bath from you sounds much sexier than from a nurse." Austin stared at him, so serious, . "Thank you for everything. I mean it, baby. You act like...like I'm worth this trouble."

His eyes rolled like thrown dice. "Dork. You are. You're mine. When I have the flu and can't take care of Rosie, you'll step up. We have this. You and me."

"I promise you that. Sickness and health, baby. And all the other things." Austin's gaze never wavered.

Damn, his heart was full. All he needed now was to get his cowboy home and his daughter in her bed. "Yes. When we get home, we'll make things official."

"We will. We'll do it up right with rings and everything." Austin snorted. "As soon as my fingers aren't too swollen to wear one."

"Sounds good to me. Momma will be over the moon." He stroked those swollen fingers. "Tomorrow night, cowboy. Then we'll be home in the Land of Enchantment."

"I can't wait, Jim. Take me home for good, huh?"

"You have my word." And this cowboy didn't lie.

Epilogue

"You about ready, cowboy?" Austin called. He would normally wear his chaps and vest and be a bull rider for Halloween, but this year it was black sweats and a sweatshirt to blend his brace and sling in, with a cape thrown over top. A tiny spot of blood at the corner of his mouth completed the look. Nothing too spooky, since they were going to the early trunk or treat for the little kids.

"I am! You want to see the cutest little bat in history?" Jim came out, wearing a top hat and a frilly shirt and a cape. That was great, but what was better? Rosie dressed like a fuzzy, sweet little bat.

She reached for him with a squeal, her little wings spreading, and he took her hand with his good one, his wrist still braced, but working pretty good now. He bent to kiss her cheek. "My best girl." God, he wanted to carry her.

She smiled at him, beaming hard. Rosie loved him as much as Jim did. She thought he was more than he actually was.

"You look pretty dapper, baby," he told Jim.

"Thanks." Jim bowed. "You look warm."

He hooted. "I am, which is good. It's cold out there." He wasn't even sorry he was missing the finals. This was the most fun he could have with his clothes on.

"Momma and Pop are meeting us at the Trunk and Treat. John'll be here in five." Jim popped Rosie in her car seat. "I figure she'll be done in an hour, and we'll pick up barbecue and everyone can come here for supper."

"Sounds good, baby." His life was this—therapy and family suppers, diapers and knowing Jim was in the bed beside him, every night. Soon he would add chores back in and breeding bulls and maybe a little arena to buck futurity bulls. But that was all window dressing. Jim and Rosie were his everything.

A year ago he thought he'd lost Jim forever.

Now he'd found everything he could ever want.

Austin had come home.

 Interested in learning more about BA's cowboys? Want free fiction and news? Join my newsletter!

About BA

Western to the bone and an unrepentant Daddy's Girl, BA Tortuga spends her days with her hounds and her beloved wife, having mother-daughter dates, and eating Mexican food. When she's not doing that, she's writing. She spends her days off watching rodeo, knitting, and surfing Pinterest in the name of research. Following their own personal joys, BA and Julia heard the call of the high desert and they now live in the New Mexico mountains. BA's personal saviors include her wife, her best friends, and coffee. Lots of coffee. Really good coffee.

Having written everything from fist-fighting cowboys to rural single dads to werewolves, BA does her damnedest to tell the stories of her heart, which is committed to giving everyone their happily ever after. With books ranging from heart-warming stories of found families, to rodeo cowboys that are fighting to make a mark, to fiery passionate love affairs, BA refuses to be pigeon-holed by anyone but the voices in her head.

Gay Romance

BA's Cozy Cowboys (cowboys w/ kids novels)

Back in the Saddle

Cowboy Haven

Cowboy in the Crosshairs

Cowboy Logic

Cowboy's Law

In the Morning Light

Ranch Manny

Security Detail: an AusTex novel

The Cowboy Contract

The Cowboy Guardian

The Meaning of Life

Trial by Fire: an AusTex novel

Two Cowboys and a Baby

Two of a Kind

The Banished Series

In Wulf's Clothing

River's Edge

Aspen's Song

The Border Crossing Series

Bombs and Guacamole

Ammo and Enchiladas

The Cereus Series

Cereus: Building

Cereus: Opening

Cereus: Training

Cereus: Rescue

The Cowboy Wanted Series

Cowboy Healing

Second Chance Cowboy

The Foster Ranch Series

The Cowboy Contract

The Cowboy Guardian

Leanin' N Ranch Series

Commitment Ranch

Finding Mr. Wright

Whiskey to Wine

Come Back Around

This Old Wind

Perfectly Seasoned

Love is Blind Series

Ever the Same

Real World

Midnight Rodeo Series

Welcome to the Pack

Tails and Whiskers

Above the Fold

Brownie's Sway

Thack's Angel

Here, Kitty Kitty

The Recovery Series

Refired

Slip

The Release Series

The Terms of Release

The Articles of Release

Catch and Release

The Road Trip Series

Racing the Moon • Steam and Sunshine

Under Pressure • Walking on the Sun

Roughstock Series

Blind Ride

And a Smile

File Gumbo

Back to Back

Pulled from All Sides

Coke's Clown

Leading the Blind

Mud, Movies, Bullets, and Bulls

Needing To

Old Town New

Rainbow Rodeo

Rough in Wranglers

Say Something

Seashores of Old Mexico

Soft Place to Fall

Stetsons and Stakeouts

Truth or Consequences

Wicked in Wranglers

Historical Standalones

Cabin Fever

Hammer and Tongs

Oranges and Peppermints

Paranormal Standalones

Baker's Dozen

Calling His Bluff

Forged in Magic

Long Black Cadillac

Luck of the Draw

Redemption's Ride

Roman and Cage

Setting His Sights

Things that Go Bump in the Night

Unearthed

Wolf Run

The Trouble with Cowboys

Hey, y'all!

Thank you for giving In the Morning Light a try. I hope you enjoyed the story, and will consider leaving a review at the eBook retailer website where you made your purchase.

Don't forget to "like" my BA Tortuga page on Facebook to keep up with new releases, author news, special discount codes and sale announcements. And if you're interested in sneak peeks, rodeo pictures, and general fun, please come see the BA's Cowboys on Facebook. We'd love to have all y'all!

Yeehaw!

BA

9 7 9 8 8 6 9 3 9 7 5 0 8